SMOKIN'

Lake Chelan Book 3

SHIRLEY PENICK

Previous books by Shirley Penick

The Rancher's Lady: A Lake Chelan novella
Hank and Ellen's story

Sawdust and Satin: Lake Chelan #1
Chris and Barbara's story

Designs on Her: Lake Chelan #2
Nolan and Kristen's story

Dedication

To the heroes in our lives. From everyday heroes (male and female) that help us over rough patches in life to the men and women risking their lives for our freedom. Thank you for your love, caring, compassion, and dedication.

SMOKIN'

CHAPTER

one

"I NEED THREE KID'S MENUS." The woman directed her three offspring to their chairs. She moved the container holding the seasonings to the side, put the sugar and sweeteners on an adjacent table, as well as the jams, took the knife out of the rolled napkins for two of the place settings and sat with a huff.

Amber smiled. "We have the children selections listed on the last page and we can scale down any of the other entrees, if needed."

"I'm not concerned about the food you are offering, I'm sure it's fine." She waved her hand as if the food was immaterial. "I need three kid's menus."

She'd already told this woman once, but she could repeat herself. "The children's choices are on the back—"

The lady turned the menu over and glared at it then turned her glare to Amber. "Are you telling me you don't have children's menus? What kind of place is this? Let me speak to your manager. Now!"

Okay this woman was starting to piss her off, but she was determined to be a professional. Amber cleared her throat. "I own this restaurant, I am the manager."

"Well, in that case, why don't you have a proper children's menu?"

"I'm sorry—"

"Like these." The woman reached into her ginormous purse and threw a dozen pieces of paper on the table. Some flew onto the floor—crayons rolled out of the papers, across the table, and onto the floor, scattering in all directions. "We've been in every restaurant between here and Bismarck, North Dakota and they all have children's menus. It gives them something to do while they wait for their food. Otherwise they make a mess and get into trouble. It's common practice. When was the last time you left this podunk town? You need to get out more. Besides that, you don't look old enough to own a restaurant. What are you? Twenty-two?"

Amber's cheeks grew hot as everyone in her restaurant stopped to watch the rude woman. She opened her mouth to say that she was twenty-five, but couldn't get any sound to come out.

From the corner booth, Jeremy put down his napkin and stood up. He walked over to the table. "Excuse me ma'am, I'm afraid it's all my fault. Amber commissioned me to create a children's menu to go along with the theme park, and I've been too busy on my book tour to get it done. I'm Jeremy Scott, the author of the Tsilly Adventure books."

Amber stood there gaping at Jeremy. Everything he'd just said was a straight out lie, except for the part about him being the Tsilly books' author and having been on a book tour. He was such a cutie, and when he turned on his charm women had no choice but to surrender to it. He had dark hair and dark eyes and Amber would bet money his body was amazing from being on the fire department. Most of the guys in town and some of the women were volunteer firefighters and she knew they kept in shape. Her brother, Chris, included. Jeremy and Chris had gone to school together from kindergarten right on through high school. He was pretty much a fixture in her restaurant for lunch and sometimes dinner, unless he was out of town on a book tour. He wasn't exactly Mr. Personality; normally he was quiet and laid back, so him coming to her rescue with such a pack of lies was totally out of character, but very much appreciated.

The woman looked awestruck. "Oh, Mr. Scott! My children love your books. I didn't mean to imply you…"

Jeremy laughed. "I have some advance copies of my latest release out in my car. How about I get your kids each a copy, to keep them occupied while they wait for their lunch? It's not exactly a children's menu, but it would serve the purpose. You go ahead and order while I run out and get them."

The woman gushed, all fight and rudeness had evaporated. "Mr. Scott that would be wonderful. Children, what do you want to eat?"

Jeremy winked at Amber as he turned to go get the books. Her cheeks heated and not from embarrassment this time. She was not going to let a wink distract her from her job. He was a cutie, but a player—he always had some new woman on his arm. Not recently that she could recall, but still. She turned toward the table and started taking orders.

∞

JEREMY HUFFED AS he jogged out to his Jeep to get the books for that obnoxious woman. Sometimes, fame came in handy. How dare that battle-ax take Amber to task. It wasn't her job to keep that woman's rugrats under control. Amber probably did need to have a children's menu, but it was rude to embarrass her, in her own restaurant. She was a hard-working business woman who kept half the town fed, and she was so darn pretty to look at. Her food was great, but he could admit to himself that watching her bustle around was a good half of the reason he ate there every day. He'd been infatuated with Amber for years— not that he would admit that to anyone.

Maybe he could draw something up for her. It wouldn't take him long. He could offer, anyway.

He grabbed his box of advanced reader copies of

his newest book, took out three, and quickly signed his name on the cover page. Then, he decided to give Amber a couple more copies she could keep on hand. In fact, maybe he should bring her over a couple copies of each of his books—to have a little lending corner to keep kids entertained. He'd have to ask her about that idea.

He got back into the restaurant and gave the obnoxious woman the three books, then turned to his table to find the biggest piece of chocolate silk pie he'd ever seen. He loved Amber's chocolate silk pie—how did she know that? Well, he did order it nearly every day, so he guessed it wasn't hard to figure out. He was going to enjoy every bite, along with the fresh cup of coffee that had also appeared while he was out at his car.

When he finished eating the chocolaty creamy goodness and could barely move, he dragged himself up to the cash register. Amber was manning it—she was such a pretty woman, with strawberry blond hair and blue eyes. Her hair had both light blond highlights and some darker—almost red—streaks. Her eyes were blue, but there was some green that radiated from the center—very pretty. She wasn't tall, more an average height, and her curves were just barely visible under the uniform she wore. No wonder the rude woman hadn't recognized her as anything but a waitress. She did dress like her staff. He wondered about that—why she didn't set herself apart in her appearance, so it was clear she was the boss.

She shook her head at him and held out her hand like a stop sign. "Your money is no good here, Jeremy. Today's lunch and maybe all your lunches for the rest of your life are on the house. Thank you so much for getting that dragon lady off my back. I owe you."

Isn't she cute. Jeremy smiled at her. "It was no big deal, and I was thinking, I could draw you up a children's menu. If you want me to."

"Oh, would you? That would be awesome." Her eyes sparkled, and she put both hands on her face like a little child would and looked at him like he was amazing.

He hoped he didn't start drooling.

"There have been other people asking for one, just never anyone quite so forceful. Someone suggested I talk to you about it a few months ago, but I didn't want to bother you."

Bother? Not likely. He would be quite happy to get her alone for a few minutes. "Oh, Amber, you're not bothering me. I would be happy to draw something up. How about we sit down and talk it over. We can brainstorm, and I can sketch out some ideas."

"Can you come in some afternoon about two? That's when the rush is over from lunch and dinner prep hasn't started." Amber caught the attention of a waitress and pointed to some customers.

Jeremy watched the exchange. She seemed aware of everything going on. Fascinating. "I can do that. I was also thinking I could leave a couple copies of my new book here for any other kids."

"That's so sweet of you—I would be honored to have them for kids to read." She took the books from him and set them down on the counter then straightened the menus next to the cash register, so there would be room for his offering.

"Great, I'll be back later with a sketchpad. Are you sure I can't pay for my lunch?" He hefted his back-pack to his shoulder.

"Absolutely. It's payment for being quick to diffuse the drama and trauma."

He laughed and walked out the door. He had something to look forward to. Working with her—not because he wanted to start anything. Amber was a beautiful woman but not his type. Well, she might be his type, but he had no idea how to approach a woman. All his relationships had been the result of women coming on to him. Shortly after high school graduation, his Tsilly books had started earning money and never stopped. Women loved him for his money. He had been thrilled to begin with; he'd always felt like a misfit before.

In school, he'd been a geeky kid who liked to draw comics. Which had been exactly what Pastor Davidson had been looking for when he'd asked him to draw the Tsilly stories that Sandy Anderson had made up. Sandy was having trouble with some of the kids she baby-sat and had used her Tsilly adventure stories to get them to behave. Only good kids got to go with Tsilly, the Lake Monster, on adventures. And some of the stories had morals to them, to teach the kids about bad behavior and the consequences of it. Pastor Davidson had heard about that and commissioned him to turn them into a flannelgraph and books to read in Sunday School. When Sandy's game won the competition, the game company had approached him and they had hooked him up with a publisher—and that was all it had taken to skyrocket his career.

From that moment forward women had come on to him—for the money to start with, but as his name got to be a household one, they had also liked the fame. Some of them had even gone on book signing tours. He'd finally realized that having them on tour was more hassle than it was worth, so he'd stopped that. Except when he was with Sheila—she had been a great organizer, and she had been an asset. Right up until she'd left him for another sugar daddy. Jeremy was tired of temporary women and their demands and drama. He'd turned down the ones that had come on to him once Sheila left; he was happily single and celibate.

At least that's what he told himself. Amber would be a completely different type of woman—a keeper, as they say, but he had no clue how to have a real relationship or even start one. So, happy and celibate was the way to go.

CHAPTER

two

AMBER WAS WORKING ON THE SCHEDULE for next week. She was out in the lunch area so she could keep an eye on the room while her staff had a meal break. She heard the bell tinkle as the door opened and Jeremy strolled in with a backpack in one hand, and a box under his other arm.

He smiled at her as he came over to the table. "Is this a good time for our talk?"

She nodded, too dumbstruck to say much. The man was a well-put together package. It always took her a minute to get her brain to function when she saw him. She hoped he didn't notice.

"It's a great time. What is all that you're carrying?"

He flushed a bit and ducked his head. "I brought in

some copies of my other books. I thought maybe you could put them on a shelf somewhere. To let kids look at when they get bored waiting for their parents. If you don't want them, that's fine too. I can take them home."

"I think that's a great idea. There are a lot of times parents want to linger over coffee or pie and the kids get restless. That's very generous of you, Jeremy."

"They were just sitting collecting dust."

"Uh huh." She barely kept from rolling her eyes at him. Silly man, collecting dust. Like he couldn't sell them in a heartbeat. She smiled at him. He was so self-depreciating toward his work. "Well I appreciate them anyway. I'll get Terry to build a bookshelf—maybe one that looks like Tsilly to draw attention. I'm sure I can find the perfect place for them. Thanks."

Jeremy nodded and cleared his throat. "So, is this a good place to brainstorm for your kids' menu?"

"Sure, we shouldn't be interrupted. My staff is having lunch, and we don't get a lot of people in to eat this time of day, on a week day. Now that schools back in session, there aren't a lot of tourists."

"Great." Jeremy set the box of books on the floor and opened his backpack. He took out a sketch pad, a notepad, a pen, pencils, colored pencils, an eraser and a pencil sharpener. Laying it all out on the table neatly, he settled into a chair and looked at her expectantly. "Let's start with the menu. What children's meals do you offer?"

"Pretty much the standard kid fare—hot dogs, chicken

nuggets, spaghetti, and mac and cheese for lunch and dinner. Pancakes, muffins, eggs, and cereal for breakfast."

"Do you do cutesy things with them, like dollar sized pancakes or smiley faces with whipped cream?"

Amber shrugged, she'd never thought to do anything like that—she'd never given kids much of a thought, at least not to entertain them. Feed them? Yes. Entertain? No. "Not so much, but that's not a bad idea. Did you have something in mind?"

"Yeah, I was kinda thinking about it and I wondered if we could come up with meal names that went along with the amusement park. Since the whole town is playing up the game and amusement park connection to draw in tourists, you should get on board with that. In fact, since it was your brother's idea to build the amusement park based on the Adventures with Tsilly game, I'm not sure how you've gotten out of it as long as you have. Hasn't Mayor Carol or Gus been in here to nag you about wearing costumes and stuff?"

Amber laughed. "Oh, believe me, we tried. But, when Barbara drew up the costume designs we didn't give enough thought to food. Serving it, cleaning it up, cooking it. We do it all day long, so the costumes were a disaster. Samantha can bake in her chef outfit in the morning behind closed doors. Then put the costumes on when she opens—to serve the rolls and donuts and coffee or whatever—without any real issues. Our first day we had open-faced turkey sandwiches with gravy as the special. The costumes had flowing sleeves. Let's just say the two did not go well together." She put her hands over her eyes and shook her head at the disaster that had been.

Jeremy laughed. "I must have been out of town and missed the show."

She nodded. "Barbara is working on some other designs for us when she has time. Right now, she's knee deep in a huge wedding, doing the bridal gown and matching dresses for something like ten attendants in all ages, shapes and sizes. After spending all summer keeping up with tourist demands for costumes to match the game. And since she's pregnant with their first child she's a little stressed, so no one is pushing her. We'll get there eventually. So, what do you have in mind?"

Jeremy had not been around many pregnant women, so he had no clue what the deal was, but he would take her word for it. "One idea was for pancakes. What if you did a little solar system of pancakes? Like different sizes for the different planets and maybe various jams to make them unique. Nothing too time consuming, but not just a plain stack of pancakes, either."

"That's a fun idea."

A slow sexy smile slid across his face, her breath caught, and her body tingled. *Bad body.*

Fortunately, he didn't notice and resumed talking. "I can't really think of anything entertaining to do with the rest of the food items other than maybe name them, like Kalar Spaghetti, or Noah Nuggets."

Amber smiled. "We could do that. Then you could

draw pictures of Kalar and Tsilly next to the food description."

"Exactly. That would take up maybe half of the page. What kind of games do you want on the rest of it? Connect the dots? Word search? A maze? Some coloring areas? Hidden pictures? A *Where's Waldo?* but with either Tsilly or Kalar?"

"Any of those would be fine."

"Yes, but we need to narrow it down and actually pick something," Jeremy said with a laugh that skittered through her body and made every nerve ending alert. He had a deep sexy laugh, more of a chuckle. She was so busy dwelling on that chuckle that she nearly didn't hear his next question. "What kinds of games did you like as a child?"

She pretended to think about that while she got her throat to start working. "I loved to color, so let's do a coloring area. And I liked to do word searches, but Chris hated them, he liked mazes. Can we do both? We also both liked *Where's Waldo?*, so how about a *Where's Tsilly?* picture."

"Alright we can do half a page of menu, half a page of *Where's Tsilly?*, half a page of coloring and quarter pages of a maze and a word search. How does that sound?" He quickly sketched what he suggested on his sketch pad— and not just some plain pencil drawing. Oh, no. He used a variety of colored pencils and a fancy pen in some places to make letters that looked like calligraphy.

She watched in awe as he worked. The man had talent

and watching his strong hands work so quickly to design the menu was not only fascinating, but kind of hot too. She wondered what those clever hands would feel like on her. She shook her head and cleared her throat. When he stopped drawing, she thought she was looking at a nearly finished product. "That looks great. Thanks, Jeremy."

"You'll need to get some crayons—you can get little four packs with your logo on them from some of those SWAG places. They should be pretty cheap, I use some of them for my author SWAG."

"What's SWAG?"

"Stuff we all get. People love to get crap with your logo on it." He shrugged.

"I don't really have a logo."

"You could maybe use the Tsilly logo if the game company released it to you—or even the amusement park one. You'd need to get permission, but since Chris is your brother I don't see that it would be a problem," Jeremy said.

She nodded and saw some of her staff coming out of the kitchen area to start prepping for the evening rush. "Not for the amusement park. Since it was our grandfather's land, he put my name on some of the incorporation papers. I'm sure he would be happy for me to advertise for him."

"You might want to get a logo of your own, too. At least eventually. If you give me your phone number or email address I can send you links to some of those companies."

Amber offered. "I'll give you both—that way we can keep in touch as needed. I can email you the list of food choices for the kids. Maybe I'll talk to Chris about it too. I would guess we might need to have a few more conversations or texts as you start working on this."

"The sooner you decide on the menu items, the sooner I'll have it done. The puzzles and games won't take me too long. Since I just got back from the book signing trip, I'll be free to work on it for a couple of days."

"I'll call Chris and see if I can get you the menu by tonight or tomorrow afternoon. Is that quick enough?" she asked.

That slow, sexy smile slid across his face again. Amber was glad she was sitting, otherwise she may have fallen from having jelly knees. "That would be just fine, Amber. This is all on your time table, so don't worry."

She sat there blinking at him for a moment, trying to get her thoughts back in order. "Well, I appreciate you taking time to work on this for me. I'm sure you have deadlines and stuff."

"Nothing pressing right now. And, I am always happy to help out a pretty lady."

Pretty? Me? Okaaay… Was he serious or just being a flirt? She had no idea. And what did it mean if he was serious? She had even less of an idea about that.

He gathered his things into his backpack and stood. "I'll get out of your hair now. When I get the first draft done, I'll be in to show you."

"I'll see you in a couple of days." She stood and held out her hand. "Thanks."

He took her small hand into his large, warm one, and

she felt tingles start from her palm and spark through her whole body.

He looked at their joined hands and then back up at her with a strange look on his face before he slowly let go of her hand, reached down, and collected his backpack. "See ya." And then he was gone before she could even think enough to say goodbye.

When he was out the door she shook her head to get the blood flowing to her brain. Wow, *Jeremy packs a punch.* Too bad she wasn't looking for a guy. She had too many secrets to get close to a man.

JEREMY WALKED OUT of the restaurant in a bit of a daze. What had just happened? One minute he was talking like a competent, intelligent adult, he'd taken her outstretched hand, and all his brain cells melted into a pile of lust. Lightning shot through him with that simple touch. She had soft skin, but also calluses—probably from waiting tables and working in the kitchen.

He'd shaken many women's hands and had never felt anything like he did holding Amber's. He wanted to pull her in, and do much more than shake hands. What was that anyway? Some kind of magnetic pull? He had no idea, but he needed to put it out of his mind. He was not interested in any magnetic pull or lust—if that's what it was. He was too damn busy for a woman. There was no way he was going to let anyone into his life to see the real him. He needed to get started on her kids' menu. Art always kept his mind clear and his emotions out.

Jeremy decided maybe he should use the amusement park and town for his *Where's Tsilly?* picture. That would be fun. He would stop by the city building to see if they had a map of the whole town he could use to get started. He could make some of the businesses stand out—like Amber's restaurant. Maybe the art gallery and the library. The landing dock, Tsilly's rock and the park where the Tsilly climbing structure was would be good. He had so many ideas.

He hoped he could figure out which locations would merit being featured over the others. He parked in front of the City courthouse building and jogged up the stairs. He wasn't quite sure where to start. So, he decided to go to the top, Mayor Carol. She knew *everything*.

Walking into the reception area, he saw her assistant take a big drink of what looked like lemonade. She swallowed and smiled at him. "Hi, Jeremy, what brings you to our humble office?"

"I was wondering if I could see Mayor Carol for a sec. If she's not busy."

"I don't think she's busy. Let me buzz her and ask."

He looked around the reception area while he waited. There were plants in corners and some magazines on the table by the waiting area, and he was surprised to see his books on another table just the right size for kids to sit at.

He didn't know the mayor had a children's waiting area. Interesting.

"Jeremy, the mayor would be happy to see you. Go on in."

"Thanks, Jennifer." He opened the door to Mayor Carol's office and poked his head in.

"Come in, Jeremy. Sit down. Can I get you something to drink?"

He shook his head and sat in the chair in front of her desk. The room had a homey feel to it. "No, I'm fine. I don't want to take up too much of your time, since I dropped by unannounced. I just have a quick question."

Her blue eyes twinkled, and she pushed a strand of her blond hair behind one ear. "You're no trouble, Jeremy. If I'm not busy with someone I have to do paperwork or email. I would much rather be interrupted."

He chuckled. "Where could I get a map of the town? I'm sure there is one somewhere, but I don't know where to start looking."

"What do you need it for?"

Jeremy squirmed under her direct gaze—those blue eyes could be piercing. "I'm going to draw up a children's menu for Amber and one of the games is going to be a *Where's Waldo?* type picture only it will be *Where's Tsilly?*. I thought using the town, along with the amusement park, would be a good place to hide Tsilly characters. I just don't want to put the streets or businesses in the wrong place."

"Then, you don't need anything technical like exact measurements or anything."

"No, just a general idea of where things are. I'm not planning to draw things to scale. In fact, I'm going to emphasize certain businesses or areas. Like the public park with the Tsilly climbing structure Kyle built, Amber's restaurant, and the amusement park—maybe the library. Things that kids would enjoy."

"I'm sure it will be clever. You're very talented. We're so proud of you and all your books."

Jeremy cringed inwardly. He knew the real truth. He was a fraud. Yes, he could draw, but none of the Tsilly stories were his brain-child. The script came from Sandy and the game company. He just drew the fairly standard pictures of Tsilly and Kalar and edited the stories down to bite-sized amounts for kids. "Thanks Mayor, but you know Sandy is the real brain behind the whole thing."

"Don't discount your abilities, Jeremy. The stories are Sandy's, yes, but you bring them alive for the children. My daughter has a vivid imagination, but she's always said you gave her stories substance when you started drawing them—long before the birth of the game."

"I guess. Anyway, about the map?"

"Oh, yes. Well, I know Gus has a nice touristy-type map that he's been working to have printed so it can be handed out at the ferry landing. It emphasizes the retail stores and tourist attractions, so it might be perfect."

"Awesome, thanks Mayor." He stood.

"You're welcome, Jeremy. Think about what I said. You are a vital part of the children's books. Without you, they would just be ideas."

Jeremy nodded to hide his embarrassment from her and walked quickly out the door. He knew some day they would all realize he was just riding the wave of fame from Sandy's game. He was a poser, pretending to be an author.

CHAPTER
three

AMBER DECIDED THAT TALKING TO Chris and Barbara at the same time would be good. Barbara had clever ideas, and they were expecting their first child soon, so their heads were wrapped up in kids. Since it was a slow night because of the potluck and bingo game at the church, she called them to see if she could stop by later.

Barbara said, "Come for dinner. We are having Nolan and Kristen over and have plenty of food for you, too. Chris put some meat in that smoker he bought, and Kristen made up a bunch of salads. I worked really hard and bought dessert from Samantha."

"Are you sure? I wanted to ask you guys about some creative ideas for the children's menu Jeremy is making for me. He wants me to think up cute names for the different meals."

Barbara squealed. "Oh! That sounds like fun. Invite Jeremy to come, too."

"I don't know about that. He's a busy guy," Amber hedged. She felt weird about inviting a man to dinner. It seemed so pushy.

"Don't be silly, he has to eat and no man is going to turn down meat from a smoker. Call him."

"I'll text him and see if he's available."

"Great. See you both about six thirty," Barbara said before she hung up.

Darn, now she had to text him. Or it might be easier to call to explain. But she didn't want to call—it seemed too forward. Maybe she could email him. And then, if he didn't want to come, he could pretend he didn't get the message. Or she could pretend he didn't get it. Yeah, email.

She carefully constructed the note to give him all the pertinent information without being too wordy. She sent it and breathed a sigh of relief. She had asked. But in a way that was not threatening. Maybe he wouldn't see it until tomorrow and she would be off the hook. Just as she thought that, her email dinged. A reply from Jeremy. Darn. She just looked at it, afraid to open it. *Come on, suck it up. He'll either say yes or no, not a big deal.*

Amber held her breath and clicked. She felt like throwing up when it said he would be happy to join the party and asked if he could bring something. How could she be both excited and terrified at the same time? She quickly typed a note indicating he didn't need to bring anything—they had it all worked out.

Now she had to decide what to wear. This was getting out of hand. The idea had originally been an after-dinner chat with her brother and now it was dinner with everyone—including the guy that made her tingle all over just from a simple touch of his hand. Well, that was going nowhere, and she was just going to ignore it. But maybe she would wear the new dress she bought—so she could show her sister-in-law. *Yeah, her sister-in-law.*

Amber drove up at almost the same time Jeremy did. What were the chances of that? Was the universe plotting against her? He got out and came over to meet her on the sidewalk. He looked good in black jeans and a long sleeved, dark blue T-shirt. His ever-present backpack was over one shoulder and there was a large bouquet of flowers in his hand. She just looked at the mums and raised an eyebrow.

He shifted from foot to foot. "My mother taught me to never show up to dinner without bringing something. But I'm a guy, so my repertoire is chips, flowers, or booze. Chips didn't seem right since you told me not to bring any food, and booze is out because of Barbara's pregnancy. So, flowers it is. They're okay, aren't they?"

"They are lovely, and Barbara will be thrilled."

The two of them walked to the front door. Amber opened it and yelled, "It's me."

Someone yelled back, "We're in the kitchen. Come on back."

Amber led the way. She wasn't sure if Jeremy had been to their house before. She went into the sunny yellow kitchen with the sunflower accents and felt her spirits lift.

Barbara's kitchen was always so fun. She hugged her sister-in-law and Kristen, Barbara's sister. "I met Jeremy on the sidewalk."

Jeremy stepped in and offered his flowers to Barbara. "Pretty flowers for a beautiful hostess."

Barbara took them and crushed them to her chest, smelling the blossoms. Then she thrust them into Kristen's hands, burst into tears, and ran out of the room.

Jeremy looked horrified. "I didn't mean to upset her."

Both Kristen and Amber patted his arms and said in unison, "Pregnancy hormones."

"But…"

Kristen said, "She'll be fine in about two minutes. She'll walk out here like nothing happened and be perfectly normal."

"Are you sure?"

Kristen nodded. "She's my sister. She's been like this for months—only a few more to go."

Just then, Barbara walked into the room and took the flowers out of Kristen's hand. "Thank you, Jeremy. They are lovely. I'll put them in some water and on the table." She turned and did exactly that.

Jeremy looked at both women and they shrugged. He cleared his throat. "I think I'll go out back and join the guys." He hot-footed it out the door.

∞

"MAN, AM I GLAD to be out here with you guys."

Nolan turned to look at him. "Why is that?"

"Oh, I brought some flowers to Barbara, as the hostess. She burst into tears and ran out of the room."

Chris groaned. "Dammit, did you have to bring flowers?"

"It was that, chips, or booze. The other two didn't seem like good choices."

"Chips would work," Chris said.

Nolan laughed and said, "Worried you're in the dog house? When's the last time you brought her flowers, big guy?"

"Shit, I can't remember, but it's clearly been too long if she burst into tears. Not that she's not doing that pretty regularly—since the second she got pregnant—but she's always been a sucker for flowers. You've doomed me, Jeremy, until I can get her some. What kind of flowers did you bring?"

Jeremy shrugged. "Just flowers—daisy looking ones, but, you know, for fall."

"Mums. Perfect, I can bring her roses and get out of the dog house. Never bring her roses. Do you understand, Jeremy? Never."

"Sure thing, man. I was just trying to be a polite guest."

"Next time." Chris pointed at him with the meat fork. "Bring chips."

CHAPTER
four

AMBER TOOK OFF HER NEW DRESS and hung it up in the closet of her apartment above the restaurant. When she had bought the business and building from the former owners, she had consolidated the four tiny apartments above the restaurant and created her large, spacious home, and a storage area. She didn't really want the hassle of renting them out and she didn't like to feel cramped, so it was a perfect solution.

Several of the other businesses on Main Street had apartments above them, like Greg's bar. Greg's was of the tiny variety and he kept it on hand for people that needed a place to crash. Her brother had used it when he and Barbara hit a snag in their marriage earlier in the year. But, they'd managed to work things out and were happily expecting their first child. Fortunately, Chris had learned not to freak out when she had her hormone explosions, which seemed to be several times a day. Barbara had given him some hassle over the flowers Jeremy had brought her and Chris had been loving to Barbara, while shooting looks at Jeremy over her head or behind her back. Amber had found it all amusing; she knew Chris would do something elaborate to get back on Barbara's good side.

She was happy with the way the evening had gone. The food was delicious. They had laughed and talked about town happenings during dinner. Then, after dinner and before dessert, they had brain-stormed for her children's menu. Jeremy had several drawings started for the other parts of the menu and everyone enjoyed looking at those and offering suggestions. Jeremy listened to each one and never seemed to get upset as they picked apart his work.

She, on the other hand, had felt defensive for him toward the others for being so critical. Some of the suggestions were good ones but some seemed kind of picky to her. He was the artist, not that bunch. She wondered if she should call or text him to apologize. The suggestion to emphasize the hotels and B&Bs on the *Where's Tsilly?* drawing was a good idea. She wanted her menu to point out all the things tourists might like.

But Chris whining about having a word search and then suggesting the maze should be bigger and the word search smaller, was over the top. Jeremy had a good eye for how things should be balanced, and Chris was just being picky because of his prejudice against word searches.

Jeremy had handled it well. He hadn't gotten upset. He'd just pointed out the balance would be off if he did as Chris suggested.

Nolan's idea was putting dots in the coloring portion of the menu, so kids could follow the pattern, one dot for red, two for blue, etc. That idea had been debated for a while, and eventually rejected—mostly because the kids would only have four crayons and that seemed like too few for that type of coloring.

They had come up with some cute ideas for the menu items and they had even suggested adding a few new items like Tsilly fish sticks and Eiffel Tower French toast. The Eiffel Tower French toast could be cut into sticks and leaned together to mimic the tower design. She knew her chef would have fun with both those additions and he would get a kick out of some of the other ideas, they had come up with for their current menu items.

Her phone chimed, announcing a text message. She picked it up and swiped the screen. It was from Jeremy.

Jeremy: Had fun tonight, thanks for inviting me.

Amber: Welcome, sorry everyone picked your ideas apart.

Jeremy: No worries, liked the input.

Amber: Anything else you need for the menu?

Jeremy: Nope, should have it done in a couple of days.

Amber: Cool

Jeremy: TTYL

Amber: Night

Jeremy: Sweet dreams.

Amber smiled as she set her phone down, plugging in the charging cord. She was looking forward to seeing the menu, but she would miss the interaction with Jeremy on a nearly daily basis. Although she was trying to resist his rugged good looks, she would miss the way he made her heart race.

Amber woke to a screeching smoke detector and couldn't breathe—smoke filled her room. She ripped her T-shirt off, grabbed the glass of water by the bed and dumped it on the T-shirt to hold over her mouth and nose so she could filter the air enough to breathe. Then, she felt for her cell phone—which she'd knocked off the bedside table. Thank God, she had plugged it in to charge. She was able to follow the cord, swipe it open and hit the emergency number even as she stumbled toward her bedroom door.

"Emergency, what is the nature of your call?"

"Smoke filling bedroom."

"I see your address on the screen, please verify." She reeled off Amber's address and her name, which she verified. "Dispatching fire department. Do you see any flames or feel any heat?"

"No."

"Can you exit the building?"

"Maybe, just got to the bedroom door."

"Stay on the line with me. Feel the door first and see if there is any heat."

She put the wet T-shirt over her shoulder and held her breath while she felt the door. "No heat."

"Stand to the side and open the door."

"Okay, did that, still no flames or heat. Going to outside door. Hard to breathe." She stumbled and almost fell, dropping her cell phone and the T-shirt. She felt around for the phone.

"Amber?"

Coughing, eyes stinging from the smoke, she ground out, "Sorry, dropped the phone. Confused. Can't breathe." *Am I going to die right here in my living room?*

Someone pounded on her door and then yelled her name. Suddenly, her door was kicked in and Jeremy crashed through it. Fresh air wafted into the room as he shone his light around to find her.

"Come on, beautiful." He scooped her up in his arms and carried her out into the sweet fresh air.

She dragged in a breath and coughed. She heard the firetrucks pull up and the men shouting but couldn't focus on it. Jeremy carried her down the stairs and away from the building to his Jeep. He opened the door and sat her on the seat. Then, he took off his bunker coat, pulled off his T-shirt, and dragged it down over her head. It was so warm. She'd forgotten she was half naked, wearing only a sports bra and pajama bottoms. Her cheeks turned hotter than the fire.

"Are you hurt?"

"No, just had trouble breathing." She coughed. "Throat hurts and eyes are stinging, but fine."

"Good. I was worried about you." He ran one finger down her cheek.

"Thanks, but I'm okay. Well, mostly, anyway." Her eyes filled with tears.

"You don't have any pets or friends spending the night that need to be gotten out, do you?"

"No, I don't have time for pets and I just spent most of the evening with you, so no hot hookups. I mean, I didn't have time to find someone or well…" She put her hands over her face. She was babbling in the midst of an emergency and he was patiently listening to her.

He laughed and pulled her hands down. "Don't worry, I understand what you're trying to say."

"It's the smoke. It made me confused." *That's a good excuse.*

"Right. You sit here and don't move until the ambulance gets here to give you some oxygen and check you out. I'm going to go help with the fire so all my work on a children's menu doesn't go up in flames, so to speak."

She nodded, looking worriedly toward her restaurant. He shut the door on the Jeep and jogged over to the firetruck.

∞

GREG ASKED, "How's Amber?"

"Coughing, sore throat, stinging eyes, but otherwise fine. Just smoke issues."

Greg nodded. "Good, glad you got here quick."

"I was still awake drawing a menu up—for Amber, in fact."

"At four AM? You are psycho. Even I was in bed, asleep, after closing up the bar."

"No, just an artist. We creative types have to work when the mojo flows." Jeremy shrugged.

"Like I said, psycho. Anyway, the ambulance will be here in a couple minutes. Go around to the back and lend a hand. The fire is all in the banquet hall. Doesn't seem to be in the main part of the restaurant. Want to keep it that way."

"You got it."

Jeremy hustled around to the back of the building, glad to be able to get into the physical fight against the fire. When the call had come in for Amber's restaurant, he'd about had a heart attack. Knowing she lived upstairs, he'd been terrified for her. He'd torn out of his house and wasn't even sure he'd shut the door in his haste to get to her. Since no one was out at four in the morning, he'd raced from the residential part of town to Main Street, hoping she was all right.

When he'd pulled up and run over to the side he was so damn glad to see the fire was showing no signs of engagement near her living area. When he'd kicked in the door he'd been surprised by the amount of smoke in her apartment. He wasn't quite sure why it was filled—with the fire on the other side of the building, that would be something to check out later.

When the fire was finally out, and they were done cleaning up, Jeremy pulled his bunker coat off.

"Whoa, what are you doing fighting a fire half naked?" Terry asked. "Didn't that coat chafe?"

Jeremy shrugged. "Yeah, a little, but Amber needed my shirt more than I did. She'd used hers to breathe through and I didn't want her getting too cold out here."

"Yeah, but a little eye candy would have been nice," the new probie said.

Jeremy grabbed him by the shirt-front and brought him in close. "We don't treat our women like that. Especially not ones that nearly died from smoke inhalation."

Terry clapped him on the shoulder. "Down, boy. Scottie here didn't mean anything by it, did you?"

Scott shook his head. "No, I was just smarting off. Sorry, Jeremy. I didn't know you and her…"

Terry clapped a hand over the kid's mouth. "Stop while you're behind Scottie and go roll up that hose."

Jeremy released him and shook his head. "Punks."

Terry nodded. "Yeah, but that doesn't mean you need to go all bat-shit crazy on the kid."

"I know. I just, well, I don't know why it pissed me off so much."

"Maybe because you're starting to have feelings for her."

"No, nothing like that. I just think she should have respect. Yeah, she's a beautiful woman, but she doesn't need the kid lusting after her."

"Well, try not to get psycho about it. He's just a kid.

When he mouths off, give him work to do and he'll learn to keep his trap shut."

Jeremy laughed. "True enough. Speaking of the woman, where is Amber?"

"Went with Chris to his house for the night. Greg kept her updated on the fire and then sent her home with Chris when it was out and he could leave."

"Oh, poor Amber. Home with the pregnant one." Jeremy shook his head sadly.

Terry laughed. "Yeah, we may need to help her escape in a few hours."

CHAPTER
five

AMBER COULDN'T SLEEP. HER MIND was whirling. She had no idea what was next. Could she get into her restaurant or her apartment? She didn't have any clothes. Maybe she could borrow some of Barbara's, but they weren't the same size. Barbara and Kristen were both pretty small women; they could nearly be twins. Amber had a couple of inches and a few more curves on her, but sweats might work until she could get some of her own stuff.

She still had on Jeremy's T-shirt and the pajama pants she'd worn to bed. The ones with the gorillas on them. She'd always loved gorillas, but hoped no one had noticed her gorilla PJs last night. They smelled like smoke, but she didn't have anything else right now. And, truth be told,

Jeremy's T-shirt made her feel safe. So, they would have to do until the world woke up and she could find out what her other options were.

Was everything roped off or just her banquet room? She was pretty sure she wouldn't be able to open until she cleaned things up a bit and aired it out. That is, if the fire department allowed her in at all. She wondered what had caused the fire in the first place—she hadn't used the room in a couple days. The more she thought about it the more questions she had.

She needed to talk to someone. Chris might know. He was a firefighter. Or Greg, since he was one of the assistant chiefs. She decided to look at email while she waited for the rest of the world to wake up—they'd all been up fighting the fire until about six and then they had all probably gone home for a few more hours' sleep. So, she didn't want to call or text anyone until at least eight or nine.

She grabbed her phone, thankful it was still charged, and was excited to find an email from Jeremy.

Hi Amber,

I rescued a few clothes for you after we got the fire out last night. I hope you don't mind me rummaging through your things, but I decided you would rather sacrifice privacy for clean clothes that don't smell too much like smoke. I put them on Chris's deck on one of the chairs under the round table. I hope they are safe. Text or email me if you need anything else, I probably won't sleep until tonight, so I'm up.

Jeremy

She was so excited to have clean clothes, she didn't give a crap if he *did* see her panties and bras. It's not like he's never seen them before—well maybe not hers, but still. She quietly crept out of the guest room, went out the back door, and found a rather large duffle bag of her clothes. It wasn't her bag, so she had to assume it was Jeremy's. She got back to her room without waking Chris or Barbara.

She opened the duffle bag and dumped it all out on the bed. He was a thorough rummager—there were underclothes, jeans, sweats, and even a couple sets of work clothes. Plus pajamas, a jacket and two pairs of shoes. There were also toiletries, tooth brush, tooth paste, lotion, antiperspirant, and her brush with some of the clips she wore sometimes to keep her hair out of her face. Her purse was also in the mix along with her cell phone charger and even her laptop. The man had some *serious* skills.

She texted him:

Amber: That's 3 times you've come to my rescue. This bag has everything!

Jeremy: I tried to think of anything you might need. 3 times?

Amber: 1.Crazy woman with 3 kids, 2.fire and smoke, 3.clothes.

Jeremy: Oh well just trying to help.

Amber: You rock. Now my hero x 3. Any idea what's next?

Jeremy: Let me call you and we can talk about it.

Amber: OK, call away.

Her phone rang seconds later. "Hi, Jeremy."

"So, what do you want to know, Amber?" His deep voice rumbled over the phone and straight to the pit of her stomach, sending tingles everywhere.

"First, how bad was the fire damage?"

"Just your banquet room. It caught some linens on fire so that's why there was so much smoke. It didn't spread to the other parts of the restaurant. The banquet room is pretty much a loss, though."

"Darn. Well, better than the whole restaurant or my apartment. How long before I can get in my apartment or open the restaurant?"

"The sequence of events is: first, we have to find out the cause. We'll be working on that later today. We did a preliminary look last night, but want to take another look in daylight. If it doesn't look like foul play, then we'll test the structure to make sure the other areas are safe. In the meantime, you'll need to call your insurance adjuster and have him do an assessment. Once he's been in you can go in. Based on his assessment you'll probably need someone to help with the cleanup. Smoke gets everywhere—like in the walls—and it might need a professional to get the smell out."

She didn't want to ask how it got started because she was afraid it would reveal too much. She couldn't think of any way it would catch on fire other than because of her secret boarder. What would she do when she was found out and more importantly how would it affect him? Poor guy. But, if she didn't ask it might look even more suspicious. "So, what did it look like started it? Bad wiring or something like that?" She knew it wasn't bad wiring, but maybe she could deflect his attention.

"I don't want to guess. We looked it over a bit last night, but we'll need to check again in the daylight."

Did he really not know or was he trying to hide it from her or catch her in a lie? "Weird, I have no idea what might have caused a fire. I'll have to ask my employees if they know anything." Her voice was so calm it even convinced her. But what she was thinking was, *Please don't let them find out.*

"Anyway, is there anything else I can help with? Anything else you need?"

Okay, no need to panic now. Just keep it light. "Other than breakfast? No, not so much. And, since my restaurant is closed. I guess I'll have to see what Chris and Barbara have here at the house." She sighed. Her poor restaurant.

Jeremy said, "Samantha's bakery is open, and I have a hankering for a cinnamon roll. Want to meet me there? I can buy you a cup of coffee and a pastry."

Was he going to grill her for more information or was this simply an invitation to breakfast? She would love a nice cup of coffee and Samantha made wonderful baked goods. Samantha was one of her best friends and she could use a friendly face, so she didn't spiral down into depression over her restaurant. "That does sound good, but I need to shower."

"I can wait. In fact, let me pick you up from Chris and Barbara's and we can go get your car after we eat. That way, you aren't stranded. How long will it take?"

That sealed it—she did need her car. "That's not a bad idea. Give me forty-five minutes."

"Done. See you at seven twenty-two."

She laughed. "Let's round that to seven-thirty."

"I'll be there at seven twenty-two, but I can wait until seven-thirty." He sighed dramatically.

She hung up the phone, laughing, and hurried to the shower—maybe she could beat him.

SHE WALKED OUT the door at seven twenty. He was already there, leaning against his Jeep, in jeans that cupped him to perfection and a dark green long-sleeved T-shirt that fit him like skin. *God, he looks good.* She wanted to lap him up. No, not going there. *Focus.* "You're early."

"So are you." A slow smile slid across his face. She faltered and almost tripped over her own feet. That smile was killer—she'd seen it before, but never specifically directed at her.

Instantly, he was by her side. "Easy there, sweetheart. Are you dizzy? Did the smoke get to you?" He took her arm and searched her eyes.

"No, I'm fine. Just a bump in the sidewalk." Her cheeks heated. *Why does he have to be so darn observant?*

"If you're sure. We can hit the clinic if you need."

"No, Jeremy I'm fine." She shook her head, frowned at him and put her hands on her hips.

He held up his hands in surrender. "So, how'd I do on the clothing selection? I tried to think of everything you might need for a couple of days."

"You did very good for a guy. It's a little freaky thinking about you going through my underwear drawer. But, better than having nothing to wear."

"Except gorilla pajamas." He smirked.

She groaned. "I hoped no one noticed." She loved funky things, but she always chose items no one else would see. To the world, she was very circumspect in appearance.

"I did, and I enjoyed rifling through your underwear—gives a man a thrill."

"I thought that was young boys."

"We never grow up in that respect." He waggled his eyebrows at her.

"Now I'm even more freaked out."

"But not as much as if you had to wear your gorilla pajamas around town."

She pointed her finger at him. "You are not a nice man."

He thumped his chest. "Sure, I am. Hero, times three—you said so yourself."

Backing her toward his Jeep, he caged her in, with her back against the door. She looked into his eyes and saw something simmering in their depths.

"Well, I may have to take it back," she said, but she sounded breathless, even to herself.

Jeremy looked at her mouth and she looked at his, then up into his eyes. He said softly, "I think I need a small reward."

"Reward?" she whispered.

He nodded a tiny bit. "Reward. Just. One. Small. Kiss." And then he leaned forward slowly, giving her plenty of time to stop him.

But she didn't want to—she *wanted* to kiss him. She'd been thinking about it for days. His lips brushed hers and she felt fire. Hotter than the fire that had burned her restaurant. And the taste of him was potent. More potent than the smoke that had filled her bedroom and a whole lot better tasting. She sighed, and he drew back. *No, not enough.*

She grabbed him by the shirt and pulled him in. This time, she pressed her lips onto his and he immediately engaged. There was heat and fire. Passion flared. She clutched his shirt like a lifeline, as he combed his hands through her hair. She had no idea how long they stood on the sidewalk in front of her brother's house locked together. It could have been minutes, or it could have been hours. But when they finally broke apart, she was stunned at the intensity of their kiss. When she finally dragged her eyes to his, his eyes were glazed and his cheeks were flushed.

CHAPTER

six

JEREMY CLEARED HIS THROAT and ran his hands through his hair. "Wow."

She sucked in air. "You can say that again."

"Amazing." He shook his head and took a deep breath. "I think it's time for a pastry and coffee. Maybe iced coffee and a frozen pastry."

She laughed. "Yeah, might not be a bad idea."

They got in the Jeep and didn't say a word as they drove to Samantha's bakery. Fortunately, it was a short drive, because she needed a distraction from her thoughts. That was a smokin' hot kiss—the likes of which she hadn't had in years. But she didn't really want to start something. And not only that, but did he think she was slutty to drag him back and kiss the stuffing out of him? He didn't seem to have minded, but she didn't want to come off too pushy.

As soon as they walked in, Samantha ran over to her and caught her up in a bear hug. "Oh, my God, are you okay? I heard you were trapped in a burning building." Samantha pulled back and looked her over from head to toe. "You look all right."

"The banquet room burned, not my apartment. There was a lot of smoke and Jeremy broke down the door and rescued me. But no, I was not trapped in a burning building and you're right. I'm fine."

"Jeremy saved you?" Samantha looked from Jeremy back to Amber.

"Yes."

"Well, Jeremy, your cinnamon roll and coffee are on the house for saving my friend here."

Jeremy shifted from foot to foot. "Samantha, anyone would have done the same."

"But you're the one who did. So, sit down and let me get your coffee and roll with extra butter. What do you want, Amber?"

"I'll have the same."

Samantha hurried off.

Amber looked at him. "A cinnamon roll with extra butter? Come here often, do you?"

He shrugged. "What can I say? I'm a creature of habit. You knew to give me chocolate French silk pie the other day."

"True. I guess you are a little predictable, and have quite the sweet tooth." *Hmm. Cinnamon roll in the morning, pie after lunch—wonder what he has for dinner. It wasn't any* of her business, but she was curious. *I'm sure he must have something.* "What is your dinner dessert?"

His ears turned red and he looked relieved when Samantha interrupted with their order, right up until she laid a baker's box on the table. "And here's some brownies for tonight. I gave you twice the normal amount."

Amber laughed. "Brownies?"

"Hey, they're delicious."

"I think almost everything Samantha makes is tasty, but..." She raised her eyebrows, teasing him.

"Eat your roll," he said mock sternly.

"Yes, sir. But first, coffee." She picked up her coffee and took a nice big drink. "Ahh, elixir of the gods."

Jeremy grinned. "Indeed. But the roll is manna from Heaven—trust me on this."

Like she'd never had one before? Silly man. She'd had dozens of them in the past for a late-night snack. Amber cut into her cinnamon roll—the smell of cinnamon wafted, and melted butter ran onto the plate. She cut off a bite and started to put it in her mouth.

Jeremy stopped her. "You have to dip it in the melted butter." He demonstrated with a bite of his own, so she followed suit.

When she put it in her mouth the flavor burst forth. Cinnamon and sugar with the warm yeasty bread. The melted butter was smooth on her tongue. She had to admit he had something. It was delicious. She moaned her enjoyment.

He shifted in his seat. "Like it?"

"Yes, it's incredible. I've had them before, but mostly later in the day when they're cold and no melted butter. They are good then, too, but I have to admit this way is amazing."

"I think so."

"Well, I guess you're more than just a pretty face—you have great taste." *Oh, God did I just tell him he was pretty?* He was, of course. And that he had great taste? She felt her cheeks heat. "Great taste in cinnamon rolls."

"And chocolate French silk pie, brownies, and pretty women."

She felt her eyes widen and her skin flush. "Jeremy, this isn't a great time for, well, for anything…"

"Don't worry. I was just teasing you. But I did enjoy the taste of that pretty woman a little while ago. I'm not gonna lie."

"It *was* delicious." She nodded and she wouldn't mind a few more samples, but it was bad timing all around. She was feeling too raw and she had too much on her plate. She wasn't great with relationships when things were smooth. Let alone when her life had just turned upside down. No, she needed to stop this idea. "But it can't really go anywhere."

"Doesn't need to go anywhere. But if it happens again, I'm not going to complain. Now eat your roll. We still need to go get your car and I can't imagine your brother is won't notice you missing."

Her phone rang, and she laughed because it was her

brother. She answered, "At Samantha's with Jeremy having coffee and then going to get my car."

"You could at least say, 'Hi,'" Chris said grumpily. "How did you know I was going to ask where you were?"

"I know you, brother dear."

"Well I made you coffee and was going to make you breakfast too, but you aren't here. How did you get with Jeremy anyway?"

Amber laughed at the suspicion in his voice. "He got some clothes out of my apartment and then left me an email offering to take me to get my car."

"Something going on between you two?"

"No, he's just being considerate, and, of course, drawing me up a children's menu." She wasn't about to mention the kiss.

"Well, as long as you're doing fine, I'm going to the amusement park this morning. I was going to offer to take you to your car, but I guess that's a moot point now. Call or text if you need me."

"Will do. Thanks, big brother."

She hung up and looked at Jeremy. "You appear to have ESP or something."

"Not really. I just know your brother."

"Yeah, I guess going to school together for a dozen years and then being on the fire department together would do that." And he's just too damn observant. She was pretty sure if she let him hang around much he would figure out there was something hinky going on in her life and she just couldn't risk it.

"Yep, you ready?"

She looked at the last little bit of cinnamon roll wistfully. "Yes. Unfortunately, I can't eat another bite."

"Great." He plucked the last bit off her plate and stuck it in his mouth.

She laughed at his audacity, finished the last drink of her coffee, and stood.

He grinned and grabbed his brownies. "Not sure what to do about missing my chocolate French silk pie this afternoon. I guess the extra brownies will have to do." He put a twenty-dollar bill on the table and they walked out into the sunshine.

They climbed in his Jeep and he started it. "I about have your menu done. I was working on it last night when the call came in."

"Oh, so you were awake and dressed. Is that how you got to my house so quick? Not that it felt very fast, when I couldn't breathe, but you made it a lot sooner than the fire trucks."

"Yeah, the rest of the volunteers had to wake up and grab clothes. And I went straight to your place—I didn't go by the department and get a truck." He shrugged and pulled out into the street. "I'm sorry you had to go through that. It's not fun."

"You've been through it before?"

"Yeah, when I was little our house caught on fire. I woke up and got scared. I hid in the closet. A firefighter found me and carried me out."

Her throat constricted thinking about him, as a child,

trapped in a burning house. Thank God, the firefighter had known to look in the closet. He could have died. She cleared her throat. "So, you joined up. To do the same."

It wasn't a question, but he answered anyway. "Seemed like the right thing to do."

"Well, for what it's worth, I am damn glad you did."

He pulled up to the stop-light and turned toward her. "Happy to be of service." He winked. "So, I'm going to go home and sleep for a couple of hours. Do you want to come by later to take a look at what I have?"

"Sleep? Now?" Was he crazy? She could no more sleep during the day than fly to the moon.

He lifted one shoulder. "We artistic types keep strange schedules. I gotta work when the inspiration is there. All those suggestions last night? I had to get them incorporated while I was still remembering and feeling everyone's enthusiasm. I used to try to keep hours like everyone else and write notes about what I wanted to do later, but when I sat down to do it, I had lost the momentum. So, I don't try to fight it anymore. I work when I need to and sleep when I'm done."

"Interesting. I had no idea. I could come over later— after you get up from your nap. Do you want to text me when you wake up?"

"Sure, maybe I could throw a steak on the grill for dinner at the same time. You up for some of Hank's prime beef?"

"I can eat some of that." They pulled into the back lot of her restaurant. She could see puddles of water and scorch marks from the fire on the outside of the building. She didn't even want to see the inside if the outside looked like this.

She looked nervously around the property to see if there were any signs of her secret. There weren't any, and she didn't know if she was glad or worried about that. She looked back at Jeremy and wondered if he could see apprehension in her face. She wasn't very good at hiding her emotions.

Maybe she could mask her concern with sadness—that feeling wasn't far away, either. "Oh, what a mess. I'm going to have my work cut out for me."

He seemed to buy it because he said, "But, not today. Let everyone do their jobs. You just need to call the insurance adjuster and wait for clearance to go back in. Take the day off today and don't worry. I'll catch you later and we can work on tweaking the menu if needed. Have a good day… since you're off work."

"Thanks, I'll see you later." She climbed out of the Jeep and walked straight to her car parked over by the stairs to her apartment. Not worry? Easy for him to say. She was worried about *everything*. She was worried about her restaurant. She was worried about the investigation. But most of all she was worried about her secret. Was he okay? Was he safe? Was he having flash backs? Would she see him again? Don't worry? Right, not happening anytime soon.

CHAPTER
seven

JEREMY WONDERED WHAT AMBER was hiding. When they pulled into the back of her place she had acted skittish, her eyes darting everywhere. She clearly had not wanted to talk about it. Of course, he wasn't saying much, either, because they had found some rather odd things in the preliminary investigation. Enough that Greg, as the commanding officer, had decided to call in someone with more experience. They wanted to make sure they followed the NFPA 921 guidelines. The National Fire Protection Association had everything outlined clearly and there were a couple of areas Greg wanted to verify. Her insurance company would want answers, and the department didn't want to drop the ball there, either.

He had to maintain his objectivity, but that kiss

threatened to burn away every thought in his head, except maybe lust. No, he wasn't going to think about that kiss— back to the fire.

An investigator was coming in from Seattle, so he would arrive tomorrow, since there was no way he could catch a ferry today. Jeremy had no idea where her insurance agent would be coming from, but probably Seattle also. So, Amber would have to chill at least today and probably tomorrow too, and then it would take her a few days with the easy cleanup. If she needed to hire someone to get rid of all the smoke odor, that might take some time. But she could be open and living in her apartment after the preliminary cleaning. Maybe a week. It might take professional fire cleaners a while to get to their remote town in eastern Washington. First, they had to get to eastern Washington. Then they had to take the ferry or barge to get uplake from Chelan.

It might take as long as a month to have it back to normal. And there was no way he was going to be able to casually go into her restaurant to see her. He would have to work out some excuses to be with her. Maybe he could help her with the cleanup. Yeah that would work. Make himself useful. He wasn't under any strict deadlines so he could spare some time. And maybe sneak in a few more kisses. *Oh, for God's sake*, couldn't he keep his mind off the woman's mouth for five minutes? He forced his mind back to logistics.

The banquet room would probably have to be completely rebuilt. She'd have to look into that after all the assessment was done. He wondered if she needed to be open to put food on the table or if she had a nest egg that would last her a couple of weeks. And what about her employees? Not that she had a lot of them. A couple of cooks, some waitresses, dishwasher, and a hostess. But, still if they were living paycheck to paycheck that would suck.

But now he needed to sleep, his eyes were gritty and his reflexes were slowing down. He dropped clothes as he walked from the door to his bedroom. He'd have to clean those up before Amber got there, but he needed to crash. He was down to his skivvies by the time he got to the bed and he dropped like a stone onto the mattress, just barely managing to draw the sheet over himself, before he was out.

When Amber got back to Chris and Barbara's house, Barbara was in the kitchen packing a lunch, getting ready to go to her bridal shop.

"There you are." Barbara stuffed a new bag of cookies into the already full lunch bag and tried to zip it closed. It wasn't happening.

"Yep, went and got my car and Jeremy got me some clothes." Amber leaned against the kitchen counter as Barbara opened the bag of cookies and dumped half of them in a plastic bag. "You don't mind if I wash the ones I was in last night, do you?"

"Of course not, *mi casa es su casa*." She said as she crammed the cookies back into the lunch bag.

"Thanks. I'm going over to Jeremy's later tonight to look at the menu. So, I won't be here for dinner."

Barbara triumphantly zipped her bulging lunch bag shut. "That's fine. Did Chris have you on tap for our dinner tonight? I know he's been picking up food from your place, rather than cooking himself. Guess we'll have to figure something else out. I'm so tired when I get home from the shop and my feet are swollen and I'm starving. Trying to cook or even think about trying to cook makes me crazy."

"Yes, I think he was planning to come by the restaurant and pick up dinner. I could whip something up for you and leave it in the fridge or even put something in the Crock-Pot. I assume you've got plenty of meat in the freezer."

"Well I don't expect you to cook, but if you want to put some meat in the slow cooker, I'm not going to throw it away."

Amber laughed. "I'll do that then. Maybe a nice roast that Chris can use for sandwiches or stew later."

"Oh goody. Thanks so much. I'm so happy to have you here for a few days. I was so scared when the call came in."

Amber watched in horror as Barbara's eyes filled with tears and she ran out of the room. She'd heard Chris talking about pregnancy hormones but hadn't been around for them much. Should she go after her? Or just wait? The night of the dinner with Jeremy, Kristen had advised waiting. Was that just yesterday? No, it seemed like at least a week. Before she could decide, Barbara walked in as if nothing had happened and resumed the conversation. It was a little freaky.

"Well, I better get going. I have a bride asking for dresses for herself and her bridesmaids and junior bridesmaids and flower girls that all match in style. Like, ten females from three to thirty all in the same style. And they are not the same shape, either, so it's quite the challenge. I'll see you later. Have a great day."

"Yeah, you too. Bye." Amber breathed a sigh of relief when she heard Barbara's car start. She had no idea how Chris handled the melt-downs, but they made her uncomfortable.

While she got the slow cooker meal ready, she worried about the fire investigation. What if they discovered her secret? She couldn't let them know—it would put him in jeopardy. She'd always hated secrets. But as an adult she realized that sometimes they were necessary.

And people that tried to ferret out what needed hiding and then broadcast it to the world just plain pissed her off. She deplored gossip and everyone in town knew it. She was often the last to know anything, even though she ran one of the most frequented restaurants in town. People knew better than to come in gossiping to her.

She needed to get online and find the phone number for her insurance agent. He should know immediately, since she was pretty sure they were based out of San Francisco. Of course, they might have a local agent that could come do the investigation. She wondered if she could come up with a plausible excuse for the anomalies the investigators were going to find.

Calls first, plotting second.

Amber spent the rest of the morning on the phone, mostly listening to elevator music interspersed with questions. But, the insurance company finally had all the information they needed, and they told her they would be there in three days. *Three days?* She couldn't even think about getting into her place for three days, and then after that he'd have to investigate and fill out mountains of paperwork.

What about her employees? Could they last a week or more without pay, or did her insurance cover that too? She could pay their base salary out of her savings, then if the insurance company paid for it she could put the money back in. But what about the tips for the wait staff? Maybe she could add a bit to their base salary. Some of them could probably get temporary work at the park, maybe. Since school was back in session, the tourist influx was slowing down. Well she didn't need to try and guess—she needed to start calling.

She was so tired of being on the darn phone by the time she was finished that she just had to cook. She didn't do idle well and talking on the phone forever was nearly the same. Since Jeremy had been her hero times three, he was going to have his very own chocolate French silk pie—and as long as she was making one, she might as well leave one for Barbara and Chris. She wondered if baby, her soon to be niece or nephew, liked chocolate as much as her brother and sister-in-law.

CHAPTER
eight

JEREMY WOKE AND LOOKED AT THE clock. Good grief, he'd slept six hours. He'd only meant to rest for a few. Damn, he probably wouldn't be able to sleep tonight, then. Which might be good, because he wasn't sure how Amber would feel about his menu and he might have to redo the whole thing. What if she thought it was crap? It wouldn't surprise him. He knew he didn't have any real talent—he was just in the right place at the right time. *All luck.* And he'd made a fortune. He felt like he'd cheated somehow, and the universe was going to smack him down one of these days for it. He was just waiting for the other shoe to drop.

But right now, he needed to shower, collect his clothes strewn across the house and see if anything else needed cleaning. He didn't want Amber to think he was a slob. He wanted to impress her or at least not scare her. Another kiss would make his day. Their first had been incredibly hot; he couldn't remember being so affected by a woman before. He didn't have time to think about kisses—he needed to focus.

He should probably make something to go with the meat. He'd have to look and see what he had on hand. He had brownies they could have for dessert, at the very least. Getting the steaks thawed out in time to grill might be a challenge. Perhaps he should put them in cold water to start thawing, first, before he did anything else.

He got the steaks in water and started to collect his clothes, then he dialed Amber to tell her what time he'd be ready for her. She'd just picked up the phone when his front doorbell rang. He looked up and saw his ex-girlfriend looking in the window. Damn, what did Sheila want now? The woman just wouldn't give up. Best to ignore her.

"Hi, Amber. So, I was thinking about six tonight. Will that work for you?" That gave him four hours to get showered and dressed.

Amber started to answer when the doorbell rang again and then a key turned in the lock.

He swore.

Amber asked, "Jeremy, is something wrong?"

"No, not really. Just a pest I need to deal with."

Sheila called out from the hallway, "Jeremy, honey, who are you talking to and why are you picking up those clothes? You don't need them."

"Sheila, not now."

Amber said, "Sheila? Your girlfriend? I thought you guys broke up. I mean someone said... Never mind. Maybe we should call this off tonight since you have company."

"No, I don't. She just showed up. We are broken up—she just doesn't get it. I didn't know she still had a key. Please come. I'm getting rid of her right now." Dammit, if Sheila screwed this up for him he was not going to be happy. What *this* was exactly, he had no idea, but he wanted to find out without interference from his ex.

"Okay, but call me if you change your mind."

"I won't. I'll see you at six."

He hung up and turned on Sheila who had started removing her clothes. Apparently totally ignoring what he'd just said on the phone in front of her. "Oh, no you don't. We are finished. Now, give me that key and get out. Dressed or not."

"Jeremy," she whined and reached out a hand toward him that he pushed away. "We're so good together. I don't want to be broken up any longer."

"No, we are not good together. You are a leech. And you should have thought about that before you moved on to that old man. That rich old man. Now, get out. Now."

"He might be rich but he's stingy. I can't even buy a new lipstick." Sheila pouted.

"Maybe you should get a job." he suggested. Like everyone else on the planet.

"Doing what?"

He said, "Um, working." That's what getting a job means.

"Again, doing what?" This time he really looked at her. She wasn't being flippant, she really was asking.

"I don't know Sheila, you did a good job planning some of my author events. You've got skills." He didn't want her to think he wanted to hire her, so he hurried on. "But my agent is doing that now, so don't get any ideas. We are not getting back together. We are not working together. It's over. Give me my key back and leave. Now."

"Fine." She flung the key at him and it hit his cheek with enough force to draw blood. Then, she stomped out of the house, slamming the door. He cringed, hoping the windows on the sides of the door would hold. Thank God, they did. He went over and locked the dead bolt, just in case. And turned toward the shower.

AMBER WAS STILL a little weirded out about the phone call from Jeremy. Was he back with Sheila? If he was, then why did he kiss her? Maybe it didn't mean anything to him. That actually might be better anyway—she wasn't ready for a romance.

She not only had a business to run, but one to rebuild. She had no idea what to do about the banquet room. Jeremy had indicated it was pretty much a loss. Did she want to rebuild? It did come in handy when people needed a place to meet and she had some groups that met in there on a regular basis. So, she should probably rebuild. Although she did wonder if the new resort on the edge of their grandpa's land could take up the slack.

Maybe it was just a friendly kiss. Although it hadn't felt friendly, it had packed a punch. And he had acted a little dazed too. Darn it she was back thinking about Jeremy again. What was that all about? Her business had burned, her secret boarder might be found out, and all she could think about was a kiss. She was clearly certifiable. She'd been kissed before and had never been obsessed by it. Maybe it was all because she'd been through a dry spell lately. Yes, that had to be it.

She'd been working hard at her business this last year, since Chris had started building the amusement park and the resort. It had brought in a ton of new people—first the construction crews and then the tourists. After that, Kristen had opened the art gallery, and the town had been flooded with people coming in to see Lucille Thompson's famous glass art and all the local artisans too.

There were only a few in-town restaurants, hers, the pizza parlor, Samantha's bakery, a tiny Korean barbeque place, and Greg's bar, which wasn't exactly a restaurant, but offered some fried foods. She had taken the brunt of the influx of people, especially for families. She had the most seating if you included both the café and the fine dining. So, she'd been too darn busy with that, and also helping out with planning for the food service in the amusement park. Thank God, she didn't have to manage those, even if she was a co-owner.

The Marquee hotel chain had stepped up to do the dining in the Resort. When Gus had first come up with the idea of a resort and forced Chris into it, Gus had suggested she open a restaurant in the hotel and even do the room service. She'd turned him down flat on the room service and then was thrilled to have the resort manage their own dining options. They had a steak house and a Tsilly, the lake monster, themed breakfast place and a quick pick up sandwich service.

So, men and a relationship had been far, far back on the back burner—like in another state far back. That was probably why she was obsessing over that kiss from Jeremy. Yeah, that had to be the reason. She certainly wasn't looking for a relationship. Nope, not her.

CHAPTER
nine

OKAY HE WAS READY, HE HAD potatoes in the oven, a salad made, the steaks—not frozen—marinated and ready to go on the grill. A bottle of wine slightly chilled and open, breathing. The table was set, and the house was picked up. He had his completed version of the menu in a folder on the table in the living room for after dinner, his backpack on the floor under the table for any corrections she asked for. He'd even set out a small plate of cheese, crackers, and grapes for an appetizer while the steaks cooked. Just call him Mr. Domestic.

The doorbell rang, and he went to answer it. And there she was, in a pretty turquoise blouse and black jeans. She'd done something with her eyes that made them pop and she had some shiny lip-gloss on that made her lips look wet and kissable. He took a deep breath, and her scent filled his lungs. He didn't know whether to pull her in his arms or run the other direction. Instead, he just stood there stupidly.

She laughed. "I brought you pie, do I get to come in?"

He shook his head, then nodded. "Yes. Of course. You brought pie?" He looked down and sure enough, there was a chocolate French silk pie in her hand. He stepped back and directed her inside.

"And I brought a jacket for later. Can I put it somewhere?"

"Yes, I'll take it and hang it up. Go on in." He reached for it and gestured toward the living room. As he turned to hang it up, he gave himself a stern talking to. *Knock it off. Stop acting like a buffoon who's never seen a woman before. She's going to think you're a lunatic or a pervert.* When he turned back, she'd taken a few steps into the living room, still holding the pie. He groaned to himself. *Take the pie, stupid.*

"Here let's put the pie in the kitchen. Does it need to go in the 'fridge?"

"Yes." She followed him into the kitchen and he put the pie in his refrigerator. "What happened to your cheek?" She stepped closer and put her hand up to the cut.

"Oh, Sheila didn't like me asking for my key back." A scratch on his face was a small price to pay for having Sheila permanently out of his life.

"I'm sorry." She said the words, but he could see her visibly relax. He wondered if she'd been worried about him going back to Sheila. That would be kinda cool if she was that invested in him.

He shrugged. "Would you like a glass of wine? I put out some cheese for a snack while the steak cooks."

"Changing the subject. Okay. A glass of wine would be nice." She picked up a grape and popped it into her mouth.

The same mouth that was all shiny and begging for a kiss. Well maybe *he* was begging for a kiss. *No. Now stop it. No mugging the pretty lady the first five minutes she's in your house.* He turned to pour the wine.

He handed her a glass and took a large drink of his own to cool off. Didn't help.

"Jeremy, you seem a little flustered and uncomfortable. Is there a problem?" Her brow furrowed. "Do you want me to leave?"

Dammit, stop acting like a jerk and relax. He chuckled and then lied through his teeth. "No, I've just not had anyone over in a while. Guess I'm having entertaining nerves."

"Don't be silly. It's just dinner and then we'll look over the menu. Think of it as a working session."

Right. A working session—when I want to kiss you senseless. Okay, not on the same page so back the fuck off, Jeremy. Now. "Want to join me on the patio while I get these on the grill? It's a nice night. We can sit out for a few minutes before the sun goes down."

"Sure, I'll bring the snacks."

AMBER WONDERED WHY Jeremy seemed so jittery. Was it really fear of entertaining or something else. Did he wish she hadn't come? Did he want to be with Sheila, but didn't want to admit it? Did he feel trapped into meeting with her to look at the menu? She had no real idea. She'd already asked once and gotten a lame answer. Should she press him or just let it go?

Or was she making him nervous? Was he thinking about *the kiss* every five seconds like she was? He looked so darn sexy, she'd gotten a whiff of him earlier, and he smelled amazing. She was working overtime to keep her distance.

For right now, she would sit on the patio, drink her wine, and have a cheese snack or grapes. Maybe he really was nervous and would calm down once the steaks were cooking. Sometimes people did get flustered over entertaining. He just didn't seem to be that kind of guy. But, she didn't know him that well, so who was she to judge?

She put the plate of appetizers on the table and sat in one of the chairs. His deck faced toward the west, so she could see the sun had just gone down behind the mountains. There were some light clouds in the sky, and with all the forest fires they'd had this summer, it was a good possibility there would be a gorgeous sunset.

She was glad the fires were finally out. They'd been

fortunate to have an early snowfall that had extinguished them last week. The hotshots that had come in were checking to make sure there wasn't anything left burning, and then they would be packing up and moving on. Fire season was over for the year. She'd heard one of the wildland firefighters, Trey, had decided to stay around a little longer due to falling in love with Mary Ann, Kristen's partner in the art gallery. It was so sweet to see the two of them together.

Jeremy sat down in the chair on the other side of the table. "Whatcha thinking about?"

She answered absently, "Trey. The forest firefighter."

"Oh, is he someone special?" he said tightly.

Is that jealousy I hear in his voice? No, that would be silly. "Not to me. You don't get out much, do you?" She shook her head and leaned back against the patio chair. "He's Mary Ann's boyfriend. I hear he's decided to stay in town during off season."

"I'm not up much on the romantic goings on in town. And I've been on a book tour for almost a month. What does he do in the off season?"

"He's a web designer. Kind of a funny combination. Geeky mixed with dangerous."

"Not too much different than me," he said with a shrug. "I write children's books and volunteer on the fire department."

"True, but nearly everyone volunteers here in town, don't they?"

"Well yeah, but everyone else isn't so geeky."

She shrugged, she didn't think of him as being geeky. But, if he did, who was she to argue. "I guess you have a point. I think a lot of people will be using him to help get their websites up to date. I know it's been one of the things Mayor Carol has been harping on, to help bring in more tourists."

"Do you have a website?"

She shook her head. "No, why would I need one? I have a listing on the town visitors' page. I think that's sufficient. Don't you?"

"Well maybe. But people do like to look into what restaurants are available in a town before they book their trips. I always look at the cities I visit as an author. They usually have a menu posted. You could have an online reservation booking tool for the fine dining area. And also, an online booking and information section for the banquet room. You also cater sometimes, that would be good to have on a website too, what you have available and how it works. Especially if Mayor Carol manages to turn this into a wedding destination place, you might need to do more catering."

So, he had a lot of opinions on this subject and he clearly wasn't thinking about kissing like she was. She wasn't sure whether to be relieved or frustrated by that. Choosing to be relieved, she said, "You do have some good points. I seem to just go with the flow of what my place has always been. Just a family restaurant with a little fancy side for the kids to take their dates to—for prom or homecoming."

Jeremy faked a hick accent and said, "Yep, time to move into this century darlin'—with children's menus, websites and all this high falutin' stuff."

Amber laughed. "Fine, I'll give Trey a call and see what he thinks."

The smoke from the grill wafted toward them and it made her stomach rumble.

He jumped up. "Good. Guess I better turn the steaks. Fortunately, I have the flame on low so I don't cremate them when I get distracted talking to the pretty lady in my home."

She blushed at the compliment. Jeremy was more than just a pretty face. He had given her something to think about—he had some brains in there to back up the looks. She glanced over to where he was manning the grill. *And a nice ass.*

While the other side cooked, they watched the sun set with magnificent reds and golds streaking across the sky. Floaty clouds turned pink and the sky darkened to purple. The smell of the steaks cooking wafted from the grill and made her stomach rumble again. She could hear some music drifting in from a neighbor's house, soft and low. The wine was from a local winery. The Chelan Valley produced some of the best wines—this one was rich and full-bodied, with just a hint of vanilla and caramel. It was a very pleasant evening, and the company wasn't half bad, either.

Jeremy removed the steaks from the grill. "Time to eat."

"Good, smelling those has made me starved."

He laughed. "All part of my evil plan."

While they ate, they talked about friends and town events. Everything was delicious. When she couldn't eat another bite, she put her fork down. "Can I help you clean up? Then can we see my menu? I have to admit, I'm excited to see it."

"Tell you what. I'm going to put these few dishes in the dishwasher and put some coffee on. While I do that, you go on into the living room. The menu is in the folder on the coffee table. Start looking it over—I put a red felt tip on the table. Circle anything that seems weird or you don't like. It will take you a few minutes to look the whole thing over, and I'll be finished before you're done."

"Alright, I'll do that. I'm too excited to see what you've done to make you let me help with cleanup."

He waved her away. "There are two plates, a salad bowl, and some silverware. How much help do you think I need?"

She laughed and headed for the living room. She grabbed the felt tip pen and the folder. There were two copies of the menu in the folder—one that was folded and one that was flat. She picked up the folded one.

On the front was a line drawing of Tsilly and Kalar standing by Tsilly's Rock with Lake Chelan in the background and the name of her restaurant in the sky with a little bird sitting on the first letter and a couple other birds flying through the air. On the ground by Kalar's feet was a squirrel, in the corner was a bunny, and a fish with a big smile on its face was jumping out of the lake. It was such a cute picture, with so many fun details for the kids to color and enjoy. She was enchanted.

She flipped it over and on the back, was the menu with drawings of the food and pictures to match the names. Many of those could be colored also and it was so well done, even the lemonade had little lemons by it and the milk had a cow.

She opened it up and there were the games. The *Where's Tsilly?* game was in color, but light enough the kids could easily circle the picture of Tsilly. Her restaurant was in the center with everything else radiating out from it. He had captured the essence Chedwick and emphasized all the major tourist attractions without taking away from the game. He'd drawn caricatures of all the people in town. She quickly found herself in front of the restaurant holding the door open for people. Jeremy was by her restaurant with a Tsilly book in one hand and a piece of pie in the other and a baker's box from Samantha's peeking out of his backpack. That made her laugh out loud.

"What's so funny?"

"You with the pie and brownies."

"Had to keep it real, and that's the real me." He shrugged.

Not many people could poke fun of themselves like he did—broadcasting to the world he had a sweet tooth. Some people were all about the front and the image they wanted people to believe. It was refreshing to see he wasn't one of them, when he so could be. With his fame and fortune, he easily could be a snob, but he wasn't. He was just himself. It made her want to snuggle into him. "Yes, it is."

She tapped the menu. "I love everything so far; the front is so cute—perfect for all ages to color. The menu is whimsical, while at the same time informative. I haven't looked at the whole *Where's Tsilly?* picture yet, or the maze or word search. I imagine the *Where's Tsilly?* picture will probably keep me busy for days, to see everything. I'll have to do the maze and word search, but I don't see a single thing I would change from this first look."

"I want you to take both copies home and continue to look them over, just in case."

"I will, but I can say right now that I love it." There was a huge grin on her face—she could feel it.

"I'm glad, but you can still make changes. In fact, I can fix things any time you want. Nothing is set in stone."

He'd already done her such a huge favor by creating it that she had no intention of making changes. "But that sounds like a lot of work for some little difference to draw this whole picture over again."

He shook his head. "No, I wouldn't redraw the whole thing. It's all on the computer now, so I would just edit the part that needs changing. Not the whole thing."

"Oh, good, then I won't feel so worried if I want to modify something. I was mostly thinking about the menu or if something in town is different."

"Exactly. Don't worry about any changes I can do them quickly and easily."

She went back to looking at the menu while Jeremy hovered. But it was hard to concentrate on the drawings when the hot guy was within kissing distance. His cologne wrapped around her, drawing her to him. She tried to ignore it and focus on the task, but her thoughts were taking a completely different path, far, far away from reviewing anything that had to do with children.

CHAPTER
ten

JEREMY WAS TENSE WHILE SHE looked over the menu. She said she loved it, but was she just being nice? He could hardly stand the uncertainty. It would be better if she took it home so he didn't have to watch her. When Amber looked up, he saw his chance. "The coffee is ready. Can we have pie now? I didn't get my afternoon fix so..."

She laughed. "Sure, you pour the coffee, and I'll cut the pie. And since the restaurant won't be back open for a few days while everyone checks out the fire, you'll have the left overs to last you."

"Thanks, but it won't be as much fun to eat it here alone rather than watching you bustle around. Half the fun is the energy of your place."

She patted him on the arm as she stood. "I'm sure you'll live without me."

The soft turquoise blouse molded to her frame and the black jeans made her legs appear a mile long. His pulse quickened and a spark of desire shot through him as she turned to walk toward the kitchen—he wasn't too sure he *would* survive without seeing her every day. He didn't realize he anticipated eating in her place as much as he did, until he couldn't. Now it felt like the week or so she would be closed was an eternity.

Following her into the kitchen, he looked at Amber again as she set the pie on the counter, and realized he really liked looking at her. The shiny stuff was gone from her mouth and he still wanted to kiss it. He was obsessed. Tearing his gaze from her lips, he looked in her eyes and saw heat shimmering there.

"Coffee. I'll get the coffee." He turned away from the temptation, toward the cupboard, but couldn't remember what he needed.

He thought he heard her mutter, "Iced coffee maybe. At least the pie is cold."

Oh, yes. Pie. They were going to have pie and coffee. He got plates down from the cupboard, a knife and spatula from the drawer, and handed them to her. Grabbing mugs, he set them by the coffee maker and asked if she took milk in her coffee.

"No just black. I learned to drink it on the run from working in a restaurant since I was sixteen. No time to fuss with cream and sugar."

"I guess I didn't know you've been working there for that long."

"Yeah, I started as a kid. I was the hostess by the time I was a senior in high school. That's why when the owners sold it a few years ago they asked me if I wanted to buy it. They even carried the loan for me, which helped because I probably wouldn't have qualified for a business loan big enough to buy the business, let alone fund the few changes I made." She handed him his plate of chocolaty goodness and he immediately forked up a bite.

"Yeah, you upgraded the menu on the fine dining side—more high end. Started carrying wine from the local wineries and Washington beers." He put the dessert in his mouth and moaned as the creamy chocolate spread across his tongue.

She ate her pie and washed it down with a sip of coffee. "Very observant of you."

"Yeah that's me—sit in the corner and watch."

She waved her fork at him. "Right, the good-looking, famous author with a woman always on his arm."

His fork stopped in midair. What? Him? He gaped at her. "Is that your perception of me?"

Shrugging she said, "Well, yeah, what else would it be?"

"How about geeky introvert?"

She laughed. "Um, yeah. No. How do you explain the beautiful women on your arm?"

"Finances, pure and simple. They like the money I make. Which is why none of them stuck around for long. They don't really like the geeky introvert, so when they find someone more fun, with more money, they move on."

"Seriously? Is that what happened with Sheila?" She set her pie on the counter and turned toward him.

"Yes. Only her current sugar daddy is rich *because* he doesn't share. She stopped by to see if I wanted to resume my role as her geeky financier. I told her no. That's when she tried to embed the key into my face. I'm just glad she didn't hit my eye when she threw it at me."

"I find it very hard to believe this. I mean, I think you're kind of hot, and that kiss? Well, I haven't stopped thinking about it." She ducked her head and looked up at him through her lashes.

"Neither have I. It did seem kind of combustible. Even in a class by itself." He set his empty plate down, edged closer to her, and lifted her chin with his hand. She gasped and licked her lips. Fire shot through him and he looked into her eyes. He saw fire burning there. He moved closer and his mouth hovered over hers for a moment, before he brushed his across hers in a soft kiss.

She moved closer deepening the caress of lips. Heat continued to build and he pressed in, licking her bottom lip. She opened for him and his tongue crept inside tasting her. She tasted like coffee and chocolate—his two favorite flavors—but she had an essence of her own as well. And that was just plain intoxicating. He felt a rumble of desire start from his mouth and move downward. He was sure he was going to explode from the pleasure, or at the very least he was overheating.

She moaned into his mouth and ran her palms up his arms and around his neck. He dragged his hands down her arms to her waist, seeking skin and found it. *So soft and warm.* His fingers caressed, drawing a shiver from her. She pulled his tongue into her mouth and sucked on it. His hands caressed higher—just below her breasts. She threaded her fingers into his hair and clutched.

Air. He needed air, but he didn't want to stop. They finally broke apart gasping for breath. Resting his forehead on hers, they dragged in oxygen.

He pulled back and looked into her eyes. She smiled. "Didn't seem geeky and introverted to me. And I'm not the least bit interested in your bank account."

"Good to know."

She sighed. "But, I think it's probably time I go back to Chris's house."

"If you must. I'd be happy to continue to show you how non-geeky and non-introverted I am."

She laughed like he'd intended. "Well as tempting as that is, I think maybe I've had enough of a demonstration for today. I did enjoy it—very much."

"I enjoyed it very much too." He waggled his eyebrows at her. "Any time you want another demonstration, I'm right here."

"Thanks. I'm kind of nervous about all this kissing stuff."

"I'm not really scary. Just someone who's lived in the same town as you his whole life, and went to school with your brother." He put his hand on her cheek. He would be happy to have her stay, but at the same time he needed to think about this a bit more. He was friends with her brother and that might be an issue. But, the real reason he was hesitant to get involved with someone long term is that she would realize he was just a poser and not a real author. She was important to him and he didn't want her to find out he was a fraud. He wasn't sure he had it in him to resist her, though.

"What about the famous author, doing book tours, going to fund-raisers, dating models?"

"That person is a myth. I'm just a small town guy who got sucked into a whirlwind. I only try to stay upright and do what my agent tells me to do."

"And the models?"

"It's all about the money. They come on to me, to see if they can get their hands on some. When it first started happening I was naïve and had no idea—I thought it was cool. Now, I'm not so naïve and it's not so cool. I want to take a step back from that person you perceive me to be and try just being a small town guy. Would you be interested in dating a small town guy?" He asked quietly.

"I haven't dated in a while and things are going to be kind of crazy right now with the mess my restaurant is in. So, you might not want to come into my crazy."

No, he *did* want to go into the crazy with her. He wanted to help. He wanted to be with her in whatever way he could. "I want to help. In fact, when you get the green light to start cleaning up, I want you to call me. So, I can help."

She shook her head. "Jeremy, it's not your responsibility."

"I know, but it's what I want to do. Now, take your

menu and look it over carefully. Call or email me with changes." Any excuse to talk to her or see her was good for him.

"Thanks, I will. It's been a fun night."

"Are you sure you don't want to take some of the pie with you to share with your brother?" He asked magnanimously.

"No, that one's all yours. I made a second one to leave with Chris and Barbara."

He got her jacket out of the closet and helped her put it on.

She turned to him. "Now be careful with your face. Don't let other old girlfriends throw keys at it." She smiled and then pulled him in by his shirt and gave him a long warm kiss before she walked out the door.

He stood there with a goofy smile on his face as she drove away. He slowly closed the door and realized she'd not given him an answer on the dating question. He wasn't sure where the idea had come from in the first place. He certainly hadn't been planning to ask her that. It had just popped out of his mouth. But once it had, he'd thought it might be a good thing. He'd never been in a relationship that he had initiated, and it felt good. Scary, but good.

CHAPTER
eleven

AMBER WOKE UP THE NEXT MORNING all hot and bothered, after spending the night in a dream induced erotic haze. What was up with that? A couple of smooches from a guy and she was a hormonal mess. Sure, they had been good kisses—in fact, they were pretty high up on the Richter scale of kisses. But still, she'd been kissed before. Granted it had been a while—long enough that she didn't want to add up the time because it might depress her. So, maybe she was due some lust in her life, but this wasn't a great time to be indulging.

She needed to nip this thing with Jeremy in the bud. She didn't have time right now and even though her body was inclined to disagree, she didn't have the inclination to make it into something.

She had to figure out what to do about the cause of the fire. She knew it had been an accident and she was a little worried about where he'd gone, if he were safe. She was certain he'd be terrified—both from the fire and fear of her reaction—since—he was so skittish.

Amber had to come up with a good story for when they asked her about the cause since she thought she was breaking the law letting him stay in the banquet room, but he'd been displaced by the forest fires this last summer and she just didn't have the heart to turn him out. The banquet room wasn't zoned for residential, although the top floor was. So, was it okay to have him there or not? Amber paced the floor. She just didn't know enough about the rules, but ratting him out wasn't in her—not when he was so afraid of everyone. What kind of story could she tell the fire inspector? She didn't want to jeopardize her insurance claim or commit fraud. What could she say that wasn't the whole truth, but wasn't a lie either? If only she could find her secret boarder to see what had really happened—and quickly. She didn't know how soon they would get back to investigating and come asking questions.

However, at this moment she needed coffee and a shower and to look at that menu, it was so cute, but she wanted to finish examining it, just in case she found an issue. Then again if she found something she would have to call Jeremy, and she didn't think she wanted to do that. She needed distance or self-control or…something. Or maybe more kisses. No—definitely not that.

She walked into the kitchen where Barbara was

munching on some toast. "Good morning Barbara, how's the baby today?"

"The baby is fine, but the mother is having severe coffee withdrawal this morning, so if you plan to have some you either need to wait until I leave or go to Samantha's. I can't bear to smell it and not have any today."

"Okay, I can wait."

Barbara smiled at her. "Dinner was delicious last night. Thanks so much for cooking. We both ate like pigs and have roast beef sandwiches for lunch, too. So, there isn't much left—maybe enough for a couple of sandwiches or some stew."

"I'll chop it up and put it in the freezer for stew later. You don't want to eat it too many days in a row. I'll think of something else for dinner tonight."

"You won't hear me complaining. I am happy to eat anything you want to cook. We still have most of the pie left. We ate too much roast to eat a lot of pie, plus I'm supposed to watch my sugar. Don't want to get gestational diabetes or anything to hurt the baby."

"No, you don't." Amber nodded. "I can do a quick run-through the house to help with any cleaning you're not feeling up to."

"Oh, that's so nice of you to offer."

"I don't have much else to do until they let me back into my place and I don't really know how to *not* work, so I don't mind." In fact, she might go nuts with nothing to do all day, every day for a week.

"Any idea how long it will take?" Barbara asked.

"Probably a week, at least."

"Yeah, that's a long time to be idle. I think I would go stir crazy. We're a lot alike in that way. Well I better get moving. This wedding I'm working on might be the death of me. See ya later."

"Bye." She waited until she heard Barbara drive off, time for coffee.

Later that morning when Amber found herself bored to tears, she had to find something to do. She'd already put together a lasagna and a salad and had baked some homemade bread for dinner tonight with Chris and Barbara. She'd cleaned the house, including both bathrooms—she figured Barb wasn't up to it these days and she wasn't sure Chris would even think about it.

She had examined the menu within an inch of its life and had found nothing but satisfaction in every one of those inches. He'd come up with so many cute observations about people in town, the locals would get a huge kick out of it. Everything he'd done was in good taste, too—no one would be upset by his portrayal of them. That was quite a talent, to do cute sketches of people that didn't offend.

She finally decided that she should go visit her outlying restaurant at the amusement park. She was only the co-owner, and she didn't go very often since she was busy with her own place, but since she wasn't yet allowed in, she could go say hi. Relieved to find something to do she headed out the door.

She was almost to the amusement park when a helicopter landed on the road in front of her. Startled, she pulled to a stop and just sat there gaping. What was a helicopter doing landing in the street? They had a heliport, why didn't it use that? The pad was mostly used for emergency transportation for injuries or severe health issues. The cost to get a flight into Chelan ran in the tens of thousands, so it was only used in dire emergencies.

The blades started to slow down, and the co-pilot got out and started walking toward her. She got out of the car and waited for the man to approach.

"Hello, miss. We were wondering if you could help us out with some directions."

"Sure, what are you looking for?" Amber said.

"We are looking for the location of the burned out home of Theodore Jordan. We understand that the snow last week finally put out the last flames and it's safe to go in."

"Yes, the forest fire is out, but I don't know Theodore Jordan?" She frowned, the only person she knew who had lived up in the mountains was Ted. Theodore? "Oh, wait there was a kid named Ted who was living in a cabin up there. Is that who you're talking about?"

"Correct, he can't tell us where it is from the air." He gestured toward the helicopter.

Out of the back jumped a young man that had very little resemblance to the homeless guy that had broken into some of the shops looking for food and camping supplies when the cabin he had shared with his father had burned. He was clean, dressed in expensive clothes, and had a good haircut. It made him look his age, which was sixteen. Before no one could tell how old he was due to his disheveled appearance.

He waved. "Hi Amber. Remember me?"

"Yes, of course, Ted. How are you?"

"Good, it's different than I'm used to, but my mother is very nice and loves me a lot. We came back to find the secret—um I mean the cross. Mom says it's a very important family heirloom and it's worth a lot of money because it's made of gold, which she tells me is the yellow metal."

"I'm glad to hear you're doing well, Ted. So, you can't find your place from the air? I know both the hotshots up at Kristen's place and the police, like Nolan, have the co-ordinates for your cabin."

Ted shook his head. "I don't know what co-ordinates are, Amber."

The co-pilot interrupted. "I do, and we saw a house on the ridge that looked like where the hotshots are working out of. Is that where they would have the co-ordinates?"

"Yes, they came across the burned out cabin while they were up there, and I know they have them recorded." Some of the hotshots had been in her restaurant one day talking about the homestead and garden they had found. That discovery is what had finally shed some light on the break-ins. Nolan had come into her restaurant asking if she had seen anyone that looked homeless and unfamiliar.

The co-pilot nodded. "Perfect. Thanks so much for your help."

"Good luck on your search and good luck to you too,

Ted. I hope you can come back and visit some time. I know Kristen and Nolan would like to see you again." He was a good kid even though he'd had a tough life.

"Thanks, Amber. I'll ask my mom about that. Bye."

She got back in her car as the blades sped up and waved as they took off. What a strange encounter—you just never know what will happen in life. She continued on to the amusement park. When she drove in, she noticed there seemed to be a lot of local cars in the parking lot. It was a school day so that seemed odd.

When she got to the restaurant she figured it out—all her lunch regulars were there. She walked in and Susan Reardon ran over to her. "Amber! Thank-you so much for coming. I don't have enough staff to handle this crowd. Most of my employees were summer kids and I just kept a skeleton crew for the winter, thinking I would only be feeding the people working on the park—not the whole town."

"You should have called me."

"I did, but just a few minutes ago when the lunch rush started."

"I must have missed it talking to the helicopter pilot." Amber shrugged.

"Helicopter pilot? I need more details on that, but not now. Can you help me get this crowd fed?" Susan begged.

"Yes, and after we get it calmed down in here a bit, I'll call up my staff and see if they can supplement your people until I get my place opened back up. Sound good?"

"Awesome. You're a life-saver." Susan squeezed her hand.

"Okay then. Let's do this thing. I'll take this half, you take that."

Amber was running around serving people when her skin started to prickle, and heat flooded her body. She slowly turned her head and saw Jeremy watching her. He was just sitting down in her side of the restaurant even though there were more tables open on the other side. She took a deep breath, finished giving the customers their food and walked over to his table.

"Hi, Amber. Didn't expect to see you here. Can't take a day off, huh?"

"Not really. I didn't expect to be put to work the minute I walked in, however." She grinned at him. "You can't seem to make yourself lunch?"

"Why would I when I can come eat someone else's cooking? Although, I do still have pie at home."

"I would hope you didn't eat the whole thing this quick." She shook her finger at him.

He grinned. "It was tempting, but I refrained."

"Good. What would you like to eat?"

His eyes heated with a thought that made her blush. She didn't know exactly what he was thinking but she had a pretty good idea. The air between them shimmered and she felt trapped in his gaze and couldn't move. Then, he shook his head and glanced down at the menu. "The chicken fried steak and iced tea. A gallon or two of iced tea—maybe enough to dunk my head in."

She laughed, and the moment was broken—and not a second too soon. While she put in his request she ordered herself to be cool as a cucumber. No flaming torch of lust for her. Cool. As. A. Cucumber.

Since it was starting to slow down a bit she let Susan finish serving and she began making phone calls to her staff to see if they wanted to work there while her place was shut down. Nearly everyone wanted to—a couple people asked for a few days off, but she managed to get a decent schedule set up to augment Susan's crew.

When she finished talking to her employees she came out of the back office to see Jeremy still sitting at his table. Darn, her stalling technique hadn't worked. She went over and sat down with him.

"Were you avoiding me?" he asked.

"Not really, I needed to get my staff scheduled in here until my place opens back up."

He just looked at her.

"And maybe I was avoiding you a little. Not a lot though, just a little. You are killing my concentration."

A slow smile spread across his face. "I am?"

She frowned at his pleasure, even as her body tingled. "It's not a good thing, Jeremy. It's a bad thing."

He shrugged. "Not from where I'm sitting."

"Changing the subject now. I looked over every inch of the menu and can find nothing you need to fix. I love it."

He grinned. "Excellent. You know, Susan doesn't have a kid's menu in here, either. Would it work for both places?

Should I design her one of her own? You co-own this one don't you? So, it's not really a competition."

"We've got a lull now—let's ask her to come talk about it. Do you have a copy with you? I didn't bring mine. I didn't think about it."

"I do."

They decided on a few changes to the games so that if the kids went to both places it would not be exactly the same. Plus, Susan wanted slightly different food choices. It would have a similar look to identify them as the same type of family restaurant, but with enough differences to give the kids new challenges. Susan didn't have a fine dining section like Amber did, the resort took that space near the amusement park. They decided to leave the "Where's Tsilly" map the same but Jeremy would hide Tsilly in some new places.

"That seems like a lot of changes. Are you sure you don't mind?" Amber asked.

"Not at all, it's only a couple of hours for me to change it. The basics are still good, I like the idea of replacing the word search with some word scrambles and tic-tac-toe spots. And I have maze generation software, so it's easy to create a unique one."

"I just don't want you to spend too much time on this and not get your children's books out. They are the most important." She noticed a strange look in his expression, but it passed so quickly she couldn't quite tell what it was.

"No worries, I've got it. But, I do think I'll get a move

on now. Susan, I'll bring you the prototype in a few days to look over. Do you want to see one too, Amber?"

"I would like to see it, but Susan has final approval since she's the one running this place."

"Great, I'll see you lovely ladies later, then."

When the door closed behind Jeremy, Susan turned to her. "I sensed some, um, tension between you two."

Ambers face flooded with heat. What could she say? There had been some scorching hot kisses but nothing really concrete was going on. "Well, I don't know what to say—we are kind of circling around each other. Testing the waters, maybe."

"Is that what you kids are calling it these days?" Susan teased.

Amber looked at her arm that did not have a watch on it. "Well, look at the time. I better get going."

Susan laughed. "Okay, we can drop the subject, Chicken Little."

CHAPTER
twelve

THE FIRE INSPECTOR CALLED THE NEXT day and asked Amber to meet him at the restaurant. She still hadn't decided what to say about the fire. She dressed as professionally as she was able between what Jeremy had brought from her apartment and what she could borrow from Barbara. Barbara's gray jacket looked nice with her black pants and white work shirt. If she wore the jacket unbuttoned, it fit well enough and it covered up the words on the shirt, so it looked more professional than her uniform shirt. She borrowed some jewelry from Barbara that Kristen had given her over the years. It was a set of blue topaz earrings and pendant.

When she arrived at her restaurant, the whole place still smelled like smoke and there were puddles of water in low spots. The door to her restaurant was open and there was yellow police tape cordoning off the back area—the access to the banquet room and the kitchen.

She was surprised to see Jeremy and Greg there with the fire investigator, standing by the front door. The fire inspector was dressed all in black and was a very imposing person, even though he wasn't particularly tall. He had a commanding aura, black hair, black eyes and mahogany colored skin. She walked toward the group of men.

"Hello, I'm Amber Clarkson." She said holding out her hand to the man, nodding at Jeremy and Greg.

He shook her hand, warm and firm. "Thank you for joining us, Amber. My name is Richard Medina, and I've been investigating your fire. We've found a few anomalies which is why I've asked Jeremy to join us as the first person to respond and Greg the assistant chief who was on the first truck and was the officer in command. I've already interviewed them and a couple of the other firefighters that were inside your banquet area during the fire."

"What kind of anomalies?" She tried to sound normal, but she was scared to death of what he might have found.

"Well one thing concerning is the amount of smoke Jeremy reports was in your apartment, even though you were on the other side of the building from the fire."

She breathed an inward sigh of relief, this question she had an answer for. "That might have been from the remodel. When I first bought this place, it had four apartments. When I had it remodeled, I left the primary space above the banquet room as a storage area and had a stair case built between the two floors from the small room in the back of the hall to the storage room on the upper floor. Could that have drawn the smoke up? I didn't have them do anything to seal off my living area from the storage space—it's pretty much a hollow wall. I didn't think insulation, or anything, was needed since it was just me up there."

"Yes, that probably is the reason. I did think that the staircase had drawn the smoke, but I didn't know the wall was hollow with nothing to keep the smoke out of your area. Hopefully you won't have another fire, but you might want to get someone in here to seal it better for the future."

She nodded. "I'll ask Marc about it. Marc is our local contractor—he did try to talk me into sealing it better when I had it remodeled, but I was on a tight budget at the time."

"Understandable, but now you have firsthand experience of why it would be better."

"Yes, if Jeremy hadn't shown up when he did…" Her throat tightened and she couldn't finish her comment.

Jeremy shook his head. "You would have made it to the door and gotten outside—you were nearly there. You wouldn't have let smoke stop you, you have a strong will to stay alive."

"Maybe." She wasn't sure she would have. Amber remembered thinking she was going to die right there in her living room.

Richard cleared his throat, bringing the attention back to him. "Another anomaly was the fire seemed to have started from a space heater and an empty chip bag. There were several empty food wrappers and an empty water bottle. Was someone in there?"

"Hmm, someone might have taken a break in there. They might have left the space heater on and didn't clean up after themselves. I'll have to ask around, I can't remember who worked that day. The fire scared pretty much everything out of my brain, but I can probably look it up on the schedule or even the receipts, to see who might have worked and then ask them." She was babbling, and she knew it, but couldn't seem to stop, because she knew it wasn't her employees that had left a mess.

The fire inspector frowned. "Well, you need to warn them about leaving trash and to make sure they turn off space heaters. The corn chips package that was near the space heater is probably what started the fire. Empty chips packages make great kindling and the table cloths and curtains probably caught from that. Unfortunately, it burned quite a while before you woke up and called emergency. The time it happened coupled with the fact this is a business district did not help in detecting the fire. If you hadn't been living upstairs, you might have lost the whole building before anyone noticed."

She laughed bitterly. "Fear and smoke inhalation versus losing the restaurant—both bad choices."

Greg said, "We're glad you're okay and didn't lose the restaurant. Both good outcomes."

"True, but since when did you become Pollyanna?" she asked Greg.

"Since I'm damn glad you are safe and sound," Greg said gruffly.

"Thanks, Greg." She felt tears threaten again and blinked them back.

"I'm going to release you back into the front part of your restaurant and your living space to start cleanup. But, I want to keep the burned out area sealed off until you find out who was back there and left the mess that started the fire. Just in case we need to do more investigation. So, I'm going to require you get wood to put over the doors and windows. So, there is no access until this is resolved. Once the banquet room is adequately secure, we'll take the tape down so you can access the kitchen storage room."

"Thanks," she said, but she wasn't off the hook yet for the fire, and that kept her on edge.

Jeremy folded his arms in front of his chest. "I'll help her get it sealed off today."

She was glad for the help, but she wasn't sure she wanted him to hang around—she needed time to think about what to do about the "employee" who had the break in her back room.

Mr. Medina continued, "You will need to wait until the insurance inspector gets here, for him to release the property, but I think you can at least get a few things out of your apartment, since it was only affected by the smoke. And you can throw out any spoiled food, but keep track of that also. I don't know what kind of insurance you have, but it might also cover that. He'll need to access your nonburned out areas for smoke cleanup costs, but it shouldn't hurt to open some windows to start airing out."

Amber nodded. "They said he'll be here in a couple of days."

"Good. I'll be back in a week to talk to whichever employee or two took their break in the room. Once we make sure it wasn't deliberate, we'll be good to go."

Amber smiled weakly. He was coming back and would need answers. What was she going to do? Right now, not panic. "Thanks so much."

CHAPTER
thirteen

GREG AND THE FIRE INVESTIGATOR left. Jeremy did not. He watched her closely. Something was not quite right about this whole situation. She seemed to be hiding something. He had no idea what it was, but she just didn't seem like her normal relaxed self. He was going to get to the bottom of this, but he hoped she would trust him enough to share what was going on. He decided to be her friend and give her a reason to have faith in him. He did want to help her.

She looked up at him and smiled, but it looked a little strained. So, he gave her a full wattage smile back. "I want to get the tape measure out of my Jeep so we can see how much wood we need to cover your windows and doors. The doors are pretty standard size, but I've never paid much attention to the windows."

"Thanks for your help, again. I'm going to put Barbara's jacket in my car, then I can dig in. I do think getting the spoiled food out of the restaurant is a good idea, don't you?"

"Yeah, do you have a notebook to keep track? It won't just be the fresh stuff—some of the dry goods might have to go, too— if the smoke got to them."

"No, I didn't think to bring a notebook. I probably have some paper in the office, even if it's only waitress pads."

"I can do better than that. I always have a new notebook or two to jot down ideas. You can have one. Hang on a sec."

WHILE JEREMY WENT to his Jeep for a tape measure and his backpack of artist supplies, Amber went into the restaurant. It looked so gloomy in the hazy light from the windows, and the whole placed reeked of smoke. What a mess her poor restaurant was in. All the cakes and pies in her Wow Case would have to go. All the salt and pepper and maybe the sugar and sweeteners would have to be replaced. The little mints she kept by the door and the toothpicks, too. The catsup and hot sauce might be fine, and maybe the little jellies and creamers. The jellies made her think of Gus and how many of them might be at his house, and that made her smile. She was always surprised that the resident millionaire stole sugar and jellies from her.

Jeremy went in and found Amber with a small smile on her face. He was relieved—he was afraid she might be crying. The immensity of a fire and the cleanup it required was often overwhelming.

"What's with the smile?" he asked.

"Just thinking about Gus and his propensity to take sugar and jellies when he could buy out the entire town."

"Yeah he's a funny old guy. Do you want me to help you get started on the tossing and recording?" She looked a little lost. He had to help her—he couldn't just leave her in this state.

She nodded. "I was planning to do it myself, but it might be good to have company—so I don't spiral into depression."

He took her hand and squeezed it. "I'm sorry you have to go through this—it's not fun. I remember when our house burned, and we lost so much. My parents nearly got divorced after it—all the anger and injustice they felt came out in the form of bickering with each other."

"I've never been through anything like this. I don't know how Kristen could be so calm during the forest fires this summer when she might have lost her house." Amber shook her head. "I'm certain I would not have been as calm as Kristen has been all these weeks."

"Yeah, but she had packed up a lot of her things while she waited for some guys to finally show up that day. So,

I don't think there was much left up there besides the furniture and house. Not that those things would be a small loss."

"No, but I get what you're saying. All my stuff is right here—both my job and my life." Her eyes filled.

Jeremy quickly changed the subject. "Yeah, do you want to be the scribe or the trash bag person?"

"I'll let you handle the trash bag, since you're a big strong guy."

"Yeah who sits on his butt and draws pictures for a living, versus the woman who runs a restaurant and carries around thirty-pound trays all day. I think you'd kick my butt in arm wrestling, but I'll man up and carry things for you little darlin.'"

She laughed as he hoped she would. They opened the windows to air the space out, while they dug in, documenting and cleaning out all the food that would be unusable after the smoke. They went through a lot of 55-gallon trash bags by the time they got the main floor finished.

When they were finally done, she collapsed onto one of the chairs.

"Is it break time?" he asked.

"Yeah I'm starving and need something to drink that's cold."

"How about you order us a pizza, and I'll go measure while we wait for it."

"I can do that. Meatlovers? And a couple of sodas?"

"Perfect. Beer would be better, but I don't think they

can deliver that. I'll be back with measurements." He walked off to the back. Once he was out of her sight, he thought about how to get her to open up about what was troubling her. Sure, she had all this mess to contend with, but there was something about the cause of the fire that just didn't sit right with him. Maybe he could get her talking over pizza.

While he measured the doors and windows he thought about what they'd found during the fire and investigation. He had been the first one on scene, but not the first one into the banquet room—he'd been taking care of Amber. By the time he got her squared away, they had the hose teams in place and were starting to get the fire under control.

Why was there a space heater in the room at all? Was it cold enough in there during open hours to need one? Why would the employees be taking a break in there rather than the kitchen or the back of the restaurant? And why would they be eating chips rather than a free meal?

He supposed it could have been a short ten or fifteen-minute break rather than a meal break and therefore just a snack. And corn chips as well as most chip-type snack wrappers, were highly combustible, with just enough oil left on the wrapper to catch fire quickly. But it still seemed like an odd location to him. He would have to ask Amber. But right now, he was starving, and he needed to finish measuring the doors and windows for the plywood to cover them.

He walked back around to the front of the restaurant

and saw she had dragged a table and a couple of chairs right next to the door, so they would have sunlight and fresh air to eat their pizza. Fortunately, there was a small breeze today, so it was helping to clear out some of the smoke smell.

"Yay, food. I thought I was going to die from hunger."

"A little dramatic, aren't you?" she said with a mock stern expression on her pretty face.

He did his best to look innocent. "Me? Dramatic? No, you must be thinking about someone else."

"Right. Well, sit down and eat before it gets cold or I eat it all myself."

"Yes, ma'am—as soon as I wash my hands. Been working hard."

He walked into the men's room to scrub up. The smoke smell was strong in there—they should probably prop the doors open to help the air circulate. While he washed his hands, he thought about the fire curiosities, but his stomach was rumbling, so eating had become a more urgent concern.

When he was half way through his second piece, he decided it was time. "So, why would one of your employees be taking a break in the banquet room? And even if they did, why clear at the back by the outside door? Seems like a long way to go to eat a bag of chips."

Amber choked on the soda she'd just taken a drink of and started coughing.

He patiently waited until she was under control. "Sorry didn't mean to make you choke. I was just thinking about it and it seemed odd. Why wouldn't they either go outside or just stay in the main part of the building?"

"They don't want to be interrupted. We don't have much time for breaks and if we stay in the room, it's hard to really relax. It can be cold outside and since the space heater was on it must have been chilly out." She said this easily, but her posture had stiffened. Her shoulders were tense, and she pushed her plate away.

"Why wouldn't they just stay in the kitchen where it's warm?"

"The kitchen is warm but never relaxing. Too much craziness going on, getting everyone fed. And I don't keep the heat on in the banquet room unless it's booked for some event. That's for your next question."

He laughed. "I did wonder." She seemed a little defensive, the answers felt rehearsed and he still wondered what was going on, but decided to back off for now. He pushed her plate back over to her. "I'm going to have one more piece and then we can head up to work on your apartment a bit. Eat up, you're going to need energy for that."

She relaxed and picked up her pizza again. He wondered if she would level with him, eventually. For right now, he was going to put his inquisitive nature aside and just be a friend. He went upstairs with her and helped a little, but once they had the food done it soon became apparent that he wasn't needed in her apartment, so decided to go get the wood to secure the doors and windows.

"I'm going to get the wood—you don't need my help up here so much."

"Okay, thanks for doing that. I appreciate you spending your day helping me with all of this. I could do it alone but being with someone else helps to alleviate the trauma."

He took her hand and drew her to him. "I'm glad I could be here for you." He kissed her forehead and turned to go.

"Jeremy?"

He turned back to her and she grabbed the front of his shirt and pulled him back to her. She put her other hand on his head and pulled him down for a scorching kiss. When she pulled back, he groaned and threaded his hands in her hair and dragged her to him. Covering her mouth with his, drinking her in like he'd been in the desert for a week with no water and she was a cool spring.

When they broke apart he smiled, looking down into her eyes that had gone blank, he kissed her nose. "You started it." Then he turned and walked out the door, leaving her standing there in a daze.

CHAPTER
fourteen

MBER STOOD WHERE JEREMY left her, staring toward the door he'd walked through. She didn't know if he'd been gone a minute, five, or an hour before her brain started working again. That man could kiss. She shook her head to try to get the blood flowing so she could think.

She kept falling back into his force field whenever they got close; she felt like an iron filing next to an enormous magnet. She wanted to plaster herself against him. This was not good—she didn't want a man in her life. Especially one who was smart enough to realize her story about the fire starting was shaky and made no sense. She needed to stay away from him before he figured out she was lying through her teeth. She wished things were different and she didn't have to hide everything. She really liked Jeremy and if she wasn't trying to protect poor Owen, she could relax and enjoy Jeremy's intelligence instead of being afraid of it. Maybe she would finish up just a bit more in here while he was at the hardware store and sneak away before he got back. Not that she could avoid him forever, but she could darn well try.

She got her suitcase out and started filling it with clothes—she was going to have to wash them all, so she might as well take them with her to keep her busy while she waited for her insurance company. She'd heard some clothes had to be soaked in vinegar to remove the smoke smell and she wanted plenty of time to work on getting it out. And it might be a good idea to know which ones were going to be a problem before the insurance guy showed up.

She decided to leave her windows open a couple of inches, so the breeze could continue to air out her living area. It wasn't supposed to rain so it should be fine. What she didn't do was go into the storage area that was on the other side directly above the banquet room. No one had told her not to but that seemed dangerous—so, for now, she would leave it alone.

She gathered up all the things she wanted to take with her and went out to put them in her car. Darn, she couldn't leave the restaurant unlocked and Jeremy needed to board up the windows from the inside. The door between the main part and the banquet room could be locked. She'd have to wait until he got there—maybe she could give him a key to lock up when he left.

She decided to scrub down tables and the counters

while she waited for him to get back. She filled up a bucket with soapy water and got out a clean sponge. Getting everything clean might take several rounds of scouring, so she would start with soap and water before she moved on to the spray they used on the tables in between customers. The table she'd cleaned off for their dinner had taken several scrubbings before the cloth stopped coming back dirty. And smoke seemed to get on all surfaces—not just the normal table top. What a mess.

Someone knocked on the open door and she wondered who it was. She didn't think Jeremy would knock and everyone else should know she was closed. She wondered if her guest had returned, but she didn't think he would come to the front door. She was certain he was hiding out after the fire, poor thing. She turned and standing in the door was Ted.

"Hi, Ted. Did you find your cabin up on the mountain?"

Ted grinned. "Yeah, we did. It wasn't easy—even with the coordinates it didn't look the same from the helicopter. The fire burned almost everything, so it all looked so different."

"Did you find the cross?"

"Yeah, want to see it?"

He pulled it out of a bag and Amber gasped. She'd been expecting a small cross with engraving, but this was huge, and it looked to be made of solid gold. It was easily six inches long and a quarter of an inch thick. He handed it to her and she nearly dropped it from the weight. "Well no wonder they wanted you to find it. This must be worth a fortune just in the gold alone."

"Yeah, I guess, but it's mostly special because of how our family got it. My mom told me it was given to my great-times-five grandfather back during the Civil War time. He knew some things about healing and saved the life of a young soldier who had been shot and not found for a couple of days. The soldier had lost some blood and was dehydrated. My great grandfather nursed him back to health and made sure he was safe with some of his own family. After the war was over the family of the boy he saved hunted him down and gave him the cross. The boy was the son of a prominent banker who had buried the bank's gold, along with his own fortune, so it wouldn't end up as spoils of war. The whole family survived the war and they were able to start the bank back up and help a lot of people rebuild. So, they felt like the gold was blessed and wanted to give some to my great grandfather. They had the cross made and then they also helped finance his dream of building a railroad."

Amber stood there listening in shock to the incredible story Ted was telling. "That's an amazing story, Ted. I'm so glad you could find it."

The boy shrugged. "Yeah, it was my good luck charm. Mama sewed it into my backpack when I was little. She told me to keep it with me and never show Pa, because it was a secret. So, I never did. I hid it from Pa, but I would hold it sometimes in the dark when I missed home."

Amber felt like bawling for the little boy taken from

his family at such a young age, but she fought the instinct. She didn't want to make Ted feel bad.

Ted ducked his head. "I wanted to give you something I made, because you helped me find it, and you were nice to me even though I stole things from you."

"But you didn't really know you were stealing, did you?"

"Well, not exactly. But I did sneak in at night when no one was around, so I kinda knew it was wrong."

"I appreciate you admitting that, but you don't need to give me anything." She didn't need to be paid for being nice to the boy; he'd had a traumatic life being stolen from home at the age of three by his father.

"But I want to, just to say thanks. It's one of my carvings, so it's not very important."

Amber smiled. She'd seen some of his sculptures and knew they were worth more than he was giving himself credit for. Kristen had sold several in her art gallery, before she knew where they had come from—and for good prices, too. "I would love to have one—the several I've seen are very well done."

"Good." He reached into his bag and drew out a figurine of a man cooking over a campfire. "I thought since you have this place that makes food for people, someone cooking would be good."

"Oh, Ted! It's awesome and to think you managed to sculpt this out of rock with the minimal tools you had up on the mountain. Well, it's just amazing. I love it."

He grinned. "I'm glad you like it."

"I do, and when I get opened back up I will put it in a special place—so everyone can see it and enjoy it."

He turned kind of pink and ducked his head. "Thanks. I gotta get going. Mom said I could only be gone for a few minutes while they get the helicopter fueled up, and my mom stops into the police station, to make sure everything is finished up."

"It was good to see you, Ted. Come back again."

"I will. Bye." He walked out and a few seconds later Jeremy walked in.

"Was that Ted I saw leaving? I didn't know he was in town."

"They came back to find the original cross that he called *The Secret*. They stopped me on the way to the amusement park the other day to ask if I knew how to find the burned out homestead. I directed them to the hotshots staying up at Kristen's. It was a little strange to have a helicopter land right in front of me on the road."

"A helicopter? Yeah, that would be different." He chuckled.

"You aren't going to believe it, but that cross was like six inches long and weighed a ton. I nearly dropped it." She shook her head.

"Oh, I believe it. I did some Internet research on Ted—when we discovered who he was. He's from a very rich and powerful family of railroad tycoons. And to think he lived his whole life up in a shack in the mountains, with no running water or electricity. His dad was portrayed as quite the scoundrel, in the accounts I read online. But, Ted seems to be a good kid."

"He is. He gave me this statue he carved. He said he thought I would like it because I feed people."

Jeremy took it from her and turned it in his hands looking it over carefully. "Hmm, kind of looks like the pictures I saw of his dad. Probably better to leave that here, than take it home. It is appropriate for your restaurant." He handed it back to her.

"I thought so. Even if it is of his dad, I love it." she said running her finger over the sculpture. "It's so amazing to think he could do this with virtually no tools."

"Well that is one thing about his father—he came from a family of artists. His father was a sculptor, and he might have passed on some information and talent to his son. He probably had a few chisels too. From what I could tell, Ted's dad never did anything of significance, except marry Ted's mother."

"Kind of a loser, but he did raise a good kid."

"Or the kid was good to begin with and just couldn't be warped by his upbringing."

"Nature versus nurture?" She raised an eyebrow.

"Exactly."

She shrugged. Who knew why people turned out the way they did? "I want to get back to Barbara's to start washing my clothes. I need to see if any of them are beyond repair before the insurance man shows up. If I give you a key can you lock up when you get finished nailing up the boards?"

He nodded. "Sure. I'm going to install a padlock on the door into the banquet room so it's secure until the insurance adjuster gets here. I'll put one on the external door, also. Just to make sure no one gets in."

CHAPTER
fifteen

THE INSURANCE INSPECTOR ARRIVED two days later. He called Amber to meet him at the restaurant. She called Jeremy to get the keys he'd used on the padlocks. He said he wasn't busy and would meet her at the restaurant, even though she volunteered to drive out to his house for them. He said it would look better for a member of the fire department to have the keys to the padlocks, so it was clear she'd not gone into the burned out area.

She wasn't sure she even wanted to see the meeting room—she thought it might depress her, but it didn't look like she would have any choice. She decided to wear one of her work uniforms; she thought it was appropriate for the meeting.

The insurance adjuster was at the restaurant when she

drove up and Jeremy drove in just a second or two after she did. Greg walked up, too. She hadn't thought about having him come as the commanding officer the night of the fire, but apparently, Jeremy had.

Amber walked up to the insurance adjuster.

He was a tall, very thin bean pole-type man with thinning blond hair and a narrow face. "Hi I'm Amber." She held out her hand and he just looked at her.

Greg and Jeremy joined them, and the insurance adjuster shook hands with both of the men and introduced himself. "Hello, gentlemen and Amber. My name is Carl Rudnick. I'm here to assess the damage and determine if my company will pay for the damages. I'll be here about a week and I will need to interview the firefighters, the investigator, Amber, and her employees. I'll need all the facts to include in my report."

If they'll pay? What did that mean? She opened her mouth to ask. But Jeremy started speaking. "Yes, sir. I'm sure you'll find everything in order. We've filled out all the paper work and Greg, my commanding officer, has followed strict protocol to ensure everything is in order for your company to assess the damage."

"Correct," Greg said. "I instructed Jeremy to assist with and document all the food removal so that it didn't cause a health hazard in our town. I believe that's the only thing that was removed from the premises except for the clothing Amber removed from her residence to wash. I also instructed Jeremy to board up all the doors and windows and he had the keys to the padlocks on the doors to the burned out area. It's all documented and the receipts kept for reimbursement."

Amber gaped at Greg. She'd never heard him say that many words all at one time; he was a quiet man who normally spoke using as few words as possible.

Mr. Rudnick frowned and said in a tight voice. "Excellent. Thank you, gentlemen. Now, Amber, you can show me around so I can assess if this is a valid claim on your part. We wouldn't want to find any insurance fraud."

Amber gasped in indignation and again opened her mouth to tell the jerk off when Jeremy interrupted a second time. "Oh, you don't need to worry about any kind of fraud—Amber herself barely survived the fire. Her home was filled with smoke when I arrived, and she was attempting to get out of the house."

Mr. Rudnick sniffed and looked down his narrow nose at her. "Well, some people go to extreme measures..."

Greg laughed and then said firmly, "You won't find any of those shenanigans in our town. Amber here is not one to do something that would endanger her life or those of anyone in our town. The fire investigator was here and found no evidence whatsoever of foul play."

Amber wasn't so sure about that, so she was glad it was Greg saying it, because she wasn't sure she could have said it and meant it. She knew it wasn't foul play, but negligence both on her part for allowing him in her room, and him for leaving the chip wrapper too near the space heater.

However, it did seem that the adjuster had it out for her—but she couldn't quite tell if it was her, or all women.

He definitely addressed the men in a more circumspect manner than he did her. So, was it her as the person with the claim he didn't like, or the fact that she was a woman. Whichever it was, she didn't like it one bit and she was going to let her insurance company know. And she needed to get the guys to stop talking over her. She knew they were trying to help—and they probably were—but still. She wasn't some fragile flower they needed to protect.

"Mr. Rudnick, I pay my insurance payments every month faithfully. This is my first time to need it and I expect you to give me the same kind of consideration that I give your company. If you are incapable of doing your job, I can call the insurance company and ask them to send out a different representative. This is not fraud. I can show you the meetings I have scheduled for that room in the next few days, weeks, and months. Plus, the revenue that I normally receive from these groups, who have standing reservations. This fire is a hardship on my business.

"The men have also pointed out that I was caught in the fire—unaware of it until the smoke detectors in my living quarters went off and by that time the smoke was thick. It was dangerous, and I was in my pajamas since it was four in the morning when I awoke. Now, if you are ready to do your job we can proceed. If you are not, I will call the insurance company." She pulled her phone out of her pocket and started scrolling.

"Well, I never… You can put your phone away, missy. I am here to do my job."

"Fine, but my name is not *missy*, it's Amber—or you can call me Ms. Clarkson if you prefer."

He sniffed. "Very well, Ms. Clarkson." Turning to Jeremy he asked, "Would you be so kind as to open the door into the banquet area?"

"By all means. Follow me." He unlocked the door and opened it to usher Mr. Rudnick in. When the man was nearly through the door, Jeremy winked at her before he followed the adjuster. Greg squeezed her shoulder, and waited for her to precede him into the room.

Amber gasped at the destruction to her poor banquet room. She was not prepared for it in any way. The tables were ruined, the little stage she had for meetings was gone, along with the podium. The walls were burned down to the outside siding and even that was warped and had holes where she could see daylight. The light fixtures dangled by threads—what was probably the electrical wiring. The ceiling was burned through in places and she could see the floor from above. "Oh, I had no idea it was this bad." Tears were welling up in her eyes and her voice came out in a choked whisper.

Mr. Rudnick turned and stared at her. "You haven't been in here since the fire?"

She shook her head and wiped away the tears that had escaped, trying to blink back the others. "No, the fire investigator didn't want me to come in. And I didn't know if it was dangerous. I've been into my apartment and the restaurant and the kitchen but not in here or the storage area above this room."

"Hrmph. Well, if you have any pictures of what this room looked like before, that would be helpful."

She took a deep breath and tried to get her mind on the question rather than the devastation surrounding her. "I might have some on my phone from when my brother first opened the amusement park. Or the newspaper might have some."

Jeremy nodded. "Yes, I think the newspaper would have some good ones." Turning to the adjuster he asked, "Would you like Amber and me to go look for some?"

Mr. Rudnick looked at Amber and then at Jeremy. "I think that might be a good idea." Turning to Greg he asked, "Can you stay in case I have questions? I assume you've been in here prior to the fire."

"Yes, I can stay and yes, I've been in here many times," Greg answered. He turned toward Jeremy with a look she couldn't interpret. "You and Amber go find as many pictures as you can from multiple viewpoints." Looking at Amber he said, "Marc built the addition, didn't he?"

She nodded.

"He probably has pictures of the construction phases and the finished product of the room. You should go ask him for his, also."

"Okay." She turned to walk out the door, then turned back. "Thanks."

JEREMY KEPT HIMSELF from touching her as they walked out of the room. He didn't want the insurance adjuster to guess they had a relationship—or whatever it was. He already thought the guy was a dick, although he did get less obnoxious when Amber was so upset seeing her burned out meeting room. It's a good thing he didn't poke at her when she was so upset, because Jeremy might have punched the guy if he hadn't backed off. He still felt like punching the guy for treating her like crap, but he could control himself.

Amber walked ahead of him toward her car. He called out to her. "Hey, let's go in my Jeep."

She stopped and shook herself before she headed toward his Jeep.

They got in and drove down the street in the opposite direction they needed to go, and she didn't even notice. He pulled into the back lot behind the fire department. When he turned off the engine, she roused and put her hand on the door to get out and then turned toward him.

"Why are we stopping here? Are there pictures here?" She looked confused.

"No, I just thought you might need a minute, away from everyone, to process."

"Process?"

"Yeah, seeing your burned out room. The insurance guy Mr. RudeDick giving you a hard time. Just life in general."

"RudeDick." She laughed. "That's a perfect name for him, isn't it?"

"I thought so, and calling him that in my mind kept me from punching him in the nose for talking to you like that. Greg was pissed off, too. Did you notice the tick in his jaw?"

"No, I didn't—and it's sweet that you guys were trying to defend me, but I can handle Mr. RudeDick myself."

"Yes, and you did a damn fine job of it, but Greg and I both care for you, and we don't like men that treat women the way he was treating you."

She nodded and tears filled her eyes. "My poor banquet room."

"Yeah, it's a disaster. Maybe I should have taken you in there before today."

She shook her head. "No, dealing with the other parts was enough. I was already feeling overwhelmed by that much. Seeing the burned out part a few days ago might have sent me over the edge. But the couple of days between revelations has allowed me to get some perspective, investigate cleaning methods, and find companies that help with this kind of thing. So, I was not so overwhelmed by the cleanup anymore. The Internet is a wonderful fount of information." She sniffed and scrubbed at the tears that had escaped. After a couple of deep breaths, she turned toward him looking less fragile than she had looked earlier.

He relaxed. She'd pulled herself out of the sadness, for now anyway. He knew it would hit again but she was a strong woman and he was going to help her as much as he could. "Yes, it is. So, are you ready to go collect pictures?"

"Do you think he was just trying to get rid of me?"

"By sending us for pictures? Maybe. I do think they are needed, but compassion might have hit him upside the head when you were so upset, and he was trying to give you a break. That's what I'm choosing to believe, anyway," he said fiercely. Because otherwise he might do something they would all regret. No, better to give the guy the benefit of the doubt.

"Well, I do hope you're right and that it wasn't a ploy to cause me more trouble."

CHAPTER

sixteen

THEY DECIDED THAT IT WOULD be easier to get someone at the newspaper that could find some pictures than it would be to track down Marc or any of his crew. She left a message for the contractor telling him what they needed and to call her back when he had the chance.

Jeremy pulled into a parking spot in front of the newspaper building and they walked into the news-room. Gus looked up from his desk, smiled and gestured them over to him.

"What can I do for you two?"

"The insurance adjuster wants pictures of the banquet room before it burned..." Her voice trailed off as tears filled her eyes. She had to stop crying, but it was so overwhelming—every time she thought of what she'd just seen she got teary.

Jeremy took her hand in his. "We were wondering if the paper had some pictures of banquets or meetings that would show not only the room, but also the stage and podium."

Gus said, "I'm sure we do. Let's go into the conference room and I'll get one of the junior reporters looking for some good ones and printing out some copies. He can also put them on a thumb drive."

"Thanks, Gus." Jeremy led her to the conference room Gus had indicated and they sat at the table. Gus came in a few minutes later with a bottle of water for each of them.

Amber was grateful for the water to help clear the lump in her throat.

Gus sat down across the table from her. "I'm glad ya came in today, Amber. I want to talk to ya about your room. I know you're upset by the fire; it's sad to see something be destroyed. But I think ya have a fine opportunity before ya, and I want ya to be thinking about it while the insurance adjuster is doing his thing."

"What's that, Gus?"

"Well ya know we've been talking about making this a wedding destination, and Mayor Carol is planning to retire next year to open her home up as a Bed and Breakfast place." She nodded, and he continued. "Well, one of the major things we need to pull that idea off is a reception hall. You've got the ground and you're going to have to rebuild, so how about ya think about rebuilding on a larger, more elaborate, scale."

"Oh! I don't know about that idea. I don't know anything about running a wedding reception." She shook her head in denial. "I don't know if I'd get enough money to rebuild on that scale. I don't know what I would even need to host wedding receptions or if I even want to. I don't know. I just don't know."

"Now, Amber. I'm not saying ya have to do it, just think about it. I could always help ya out with the finances. And maybe one of the folks in town has some skills that could help ya out with the planning and execution of the events. Ya could maybe just rent out the space and do the catering."

"But why wouldn't people use the resort?"

"Some of them will, but the Marquee Resorts only have specific packages that they offer for weddings. People that want something different than what they offer would be your customers."

"But—"

"Here's young Craig with your pictures. Now you just think on what I said. No need to decide today. I'm just going to mosey along, now. Good day to ya." He walked out of the room and Craig walked in.

"Hey, Amber. Sorry about your place, man that was quite the fire. Your brother and I were right in the thick of it. Those curtains and table-cloths made that place look like a fire right from the bowels of hell. Well, probably not as bad as those fire jumpers and hotshots on the mountain are used to, but bigger than I've ever been a part of. Hey, Jeremy. How's it hanging man?"

Amber smiled at Craig. The guy had been a fixture at their house growing up and was always gregarious.

"I'm good, Craig. Thanks for looking up those pictures for Amber."

"Oh, right. The pictures. Well, here they are. I hope they're what you're looking for."

Jeremy flipped through the pictures. "They look perfect, Craig. Thanks." He handed them to her and she looked through them, too. But her mind was whirling with what Gus had suggested. She didn't really see a single picture—she'd have to trust Jeremy that they were what they needed.

She smiled at Craig. "Thanks, Craig, we need to get going. See you later."

"Yep, I'll be back into the restaurant as soon as you get it re-opened. I am sick to death of my own cooking. Maybe it's time I settled down and get me a wife who can cook."

She rolled her eyes at him and she heard him laugh as they left the room.

When they got to Jeremy's Jeep, she got in and said, "Just drive—anywhere not around people." She had no idea where he was going; she couldn't focus on anything as mundane as their location. When he turned off the engine she looked out and noticed they were at Kissing Cove.

"Seriously? Kissing Cove?"

"Hey, no one is going to bother anyone at Kissing Cove in the daylight. So, talk to me."

"He wants me to build a wedding reception venue. Do you have any idea what that would entail? I would need not only a huge banquet room, but also changing rooms, and more buffet space, and room for a cake, and a dance floor, and a high-end sound system, and a pretty entrance without them having to go through the restaurant, and better parking, and a projection system. Is he fricken' crazy?

"And that's just the physical issues, let alone the logistics. Wedding reception co-ordination is a huge job, and these brides flying in for a destination wedding are going to assume we have someone handling all that. They sure as heck aren't going to be bringing someone with them to figure it all out. And I don't have time for all that crap. I've got the restaurant to run, both the café side and the fine dining. I've got a hand in the one at the amusement park, and now he wants me to do wedding receptions? No, I won't be railroaded into this." She folded her arms across her chest with a fierce expression on her face.

She shook her finger him. "You know he's sneaky, going around roping people into things they never wanted in the first place, like the resort on Chris's land, and the art gallery at Kristen's, and now he's strong-arming me into a wedding reception venue." She slumped back into her seat.

Jeremy looked at her. "I will back you up with whatever decision you make. And it's your decision to make, not Gus's."

"Thanks, Jeremy." She leaned over and put her head on his shoulder.

"I don't want to see you stressing about this." He took her hand and brought it to his mouth and kissed her knuckles.

"This is nice. Can we just sit here for a week—or maybe two—and ignore the world?" As soon as she finished speaking her phone rang. She groaned. "Guess not. Had to jinx it didn't I." She looked at the screen, and answered, "Hi Marc." When she got off the phone, she told Jeremy, "Marc's going to meet us at the restaurant. He has some pictures for the insurance guy. Relaxing time is over."

When they got to the restaurant, they gave Mr. RudeDick the pictures from the newspaper and Marc gave him the pictures he had.

"Very good. I've finished my inspection, and I'll get this written up and turned in. You should receive a check in a few weeks. You can go ahead and start cleaning it up to reopen at your convenience."

Amber gaped at him. "That's it? No questions?" He wasn't going to ask her how the fire had started? She wasn't going to have to perpetuate the lame excuse she'd told the fire investigator?

"Yes, I'm quite finished and Greg's informed me that the late ferry will be by in an hour, so I am going to take advantage of that." He shook hands with each of them, including her, and then walked away.

They all stood there watching him leave, and when he'd

gone, Jeremy turned to Greg and asked, "What did you do? Threaten to slice him up and feed him to the fishes?"

"Nothing quite so dramatic. I just gave him a few pointers on how things work in small towns."

Amber, who had been staring in the direction the insurance man had taken, slowly turned her head to look at Greg. "You threatened him?"

"Nope," he said and then crossed his arms over his chest, which indicated he was finished with the subject. But there was a twinkle in his eye.

CHAPTER
seventeen

AMBER WAS SO HAPPY TO BE able to get back into her restaurant. She called her staff to see, who wanted back on the payroll at a special cleaning rate higher than their normal salary. She called some professional people who could remove the smoke smells trapped in the walls. Jeremy was on hand to assist. Samantha came by when the bakery closed. Chris was there to help when he wasn't needed at the amusement park. Greg came by in the mornings and afternoons before the bar opened. Nearly everyone in town showed up at one time or another to lend a hand. She had so much assistance she ended up directing people most of the time, and doing very little of the actual work.

One afternoon when they were nearly ready to reopen,

Mayor Carol walked in. "Well, this is looking very nice. Did you repaint?"

"Yes, it seemed like a good time. I had been thinking about it for a while, but just couldn't figure out how to do it without closing. But since I was already closed…"

"It's lovely and fresh."

"I used the color scheme from before and just added a few accents in phthalo blue, to make it pop."

"Interesting color choice, but it does feel brighter now. Can you leave for a few minutes? I'd like you to take a walk with me."

"Um, sure." She had no idea what the mayor wanted, but she wasn't going to turn her down. Looking around, she caught Jeremy's eye. "Jeremy, can you manage this crew?"

"You got it, boss."

They walked down the street and Mayor Carol talked about random topics, which caused Amber to wonder what the point of this was. When they reached Samantha's bakery she said, "Let's go in here and get a cup of coffee."

"Samantha's not usually open this late."

"She is today."

Amber knew she'd been ambushed the minute she walked in. Samantha was there. Samantha, who made wedding cakes, and Mayor Carol who was turning her home into a B&B, and was the instigator of the wedding destination idea. Barbara and her partners who made wedding dresses were also present. Kendra who maintained the wedding chapel, and Laura, who had a flower shop, and a couple of the other B&B owners stood sipping coffee and looking at them expectantly.

She groaned and sat down. "This is an intervention, isn't it?"

"Not at all, dear. Iit's just a few of your fellow townspeople wanting to share their ideas with you."

"Well, it feels like an ambush. Did Gus talk you into this?" She put her hands on her hips.

Mayor Carol shook her head. "No, Gus has nothing to do with it. I felt like it was time to start working on the wedding destination idea the town came up with during our brainstorming session in January. We already have the other two ideas well in hand."

Laura nodded. "I agree we need to start making plans. Mayor Carol will be putting all her eggs in one basket starting next fall and we should have things in place before then. Brides start planning weddings far in advance, so we need to start advertising, but we can't do that until we have the full package."

"But I don't know if I want to be a part of it." Amber folded her arms protectively across her chest. "I know I need to rebuild, but a banquet and meeting room is a far cry from what a wedding reception venue requires."

Barbara gasped. "I was invited to a meeting to discuss making our town a wedding destination, and I had no idea it was a meeting to convince you to build a reception venue. I don't appreciate being railroaded any more than you do. I'm so sorry, Amber. I think this was very mean." Barbara said as tears filled her eyes, and she ran out of the room.

"Oh, my. I'm not that upset, I should go after her…" Amber started to stand.

Christa stopped her. "No, wait. You know the drill by now. Give her five minutes—it's just the pregnancy hormones. She'll be back, and she'll act like nothing happened. Trust me on this."

Amber sat back down but looked toward the ladies room where Barbara had gone. "Yeah, I've seen it before. But if she isn't back in five minutes, I'm going after her."

Mayor Carol spoke. "Now, as far as being ambushed, Amber, you've always had the only room large enough to host a wedding reception, so you would have been invited to this to determine your interest anyway."

"Oh, I didn't think about that. It's just that Gus already talked to me about it, and I felt he was giving me the strong arm like he did Chris and Kristen."

"That's not a big surprise, and even you have to admit that those times he did do that have worked out well." Amber saw Barbara come out of the bathroom as Mayor Carol continued. "Now, the fact that you must rebuild and have the potential to make it a first-class wedding reception venue is just icing on the cake, if you chose to do it. No one is here to railroad you into anything—it is your choice. We are here to have a discussion about what we see as roadblocks and opportunities to make our town a wedding destination."

Turning to Barbara she asked, "Is that more what you thought you were invited for?"

"Yes, thank you for explaining."

Mayor Carol returned her focus to Amber. "Do you wish to stay and participate?"

"Yes, I do. But I still haven't decided on anything. Partly because I don't feel qualified or capable of managing wedding receptions."

"I don't think anyone is expecting you to be a wedding reception planner or to execute them." Mayor Carol paused as the door opened and Sheila rushed in. "And here is Sheila, right on time. She is the one Gus and I decided would be willing and capable to be the wedding planner."

Sheila said, "Sorry I'm late I was working with Kyle on a rental property. I'm going to move into. Now that I have a job, I'm able to do that." She beamed at the group.

"I'm so excited, I've never been paid to put on these types of events. I've always done them for free." She blushed, ducked her head, and said, "Well, not paid in the normal way."

Mayor Carol waved her hand. "Being the hostess and planning large events for one's companion has always been a normal, and often expected, part of a relationship. Now, let's move on."

Sheila sat up a little straighter at that and Amber found that very interesting. This was a side of Sheila's personality she had never seen. She wondered how the two of them would work together if she did rebuild on a larger scale.

As the meeting wore on, a lot of good ideas surfaced, and plans were made. Sheila contributed so much to the meeting that Amber was fascinated to see this aspect of the woman. She was intelligent, well spoken, and knowledgeable about events and the requirements to host them. Why hadn't she known Sheila was like this before? She'd always just seen the woman as arm candy for whatever man she was with at the time.

The more they talked the more it became apparent that they really did need a reception venue. Amber felt more and more like a jerk to be holding back, but she needed a lot more information—and a lot more time—to think about it all.

CHAPTER
eighteen

JEREMY WAS RELIEVED WHEN AMBER finally got back to the restaurant. He had no idea why Mayor Carol would take Amber away in the middle of cleaning and repairing and then keep her for over an hour and a half. He hoped everything was all right. She came over to him looking kind of tense.

"Everything okay?" He asked.

"Sure. Just dandy."

Uh oh. He took her by the hand and led her back to her office and closed the door. At least this room was finished and didn't smell like smoke—those professional cleaners did a good job.

"So, what's wrong?"

She sighed. "Nothing really. I just feel trapped. Mayor

Carol wanted me to be a part of a meeting on making Chedwick a wedding destination. It's been an idea all year, but she wanted to make some concrete plans. Which is all well and good, but the major missing piece is a reception venue. And who could possibly do that except me?"

"You do have the space and the opportunity."

"Yeah, but I know nothing—less than nothing—about it. Mayor Carol was ready for that, though. She and Gus hired Sheila to be the town wedding planner, or set her up with her own business or something."

"Sheila? As in my old girlfriend?" He looked at Amber and she nodded. "Well I guess that would make sense. She's really good at planning and organizing events. Much better than my agent and the yahoos they hire to do book launch parties. When Sheila and I were together she did a darn good job with things like that."

"I noticed. During the meeting, she was the one that had the most knowledge and gave the best suggestions. Everything from advertising and where to do that, to the best place to buy voile. She had more research information than even Barbara did on fabric. She blew me away."

"So, if Sheila is going to do the planning and execution what is your concern?" Jeremy asked.

"It just seems like such a huge commitment. If I go all-in with this idea and build a fancy reception venue, then my work will increase. What if we have a wedding every weekend—or two or more on a weekend. We'd have increased kitchen traffic and I'd have to hire more staff—people who know how to do weddings. Right now, I use that room a few times a month. This would increase it to a few times a week. That's a lot of work."

"But it would also be a significant increase in revenue, wouldn't it?"

"Yes—of course it would. But is it worth a seventy-hour work week?"

Jeremy took her hand. "Playing the devil's advocate here. Could you hire someone else to manage it? Wouldn't that be Sheila's job?"

"No, she would manage the wedding and reception, but not the catering or the facility." She shook her head and then stilled. Jeremy waited to see what would come next. "But maybe I could find someone to help with the catering and the facility. It's something to think about."

He nodded, but then said firmly, "I think whatever you decide, it's still your life and your property."

"Yeah, I know. But I hate being the broken cog in the wheel."

"You aren't broken—you're just counting the cost instead of jumping on the bandwagon. A smart move on your part. You have to do what's right for you—the town will find another way if they need to. You doing it reluctantly will be evident to people, it will cause them to feel uncomfortable. So, you have to be on board with it one hundred percent before you commit."

"Thanks, Jeremy. I don't know if I'll ever get to one hundred percent, but I might get to ninety or ninety-five." She gave him a lopsided smile.

"I think that would work, but it's your life and your

business and you need to stand firm on what you want. I'll be right there with you supporting your decision." He took her other hand and held them in his, rubbing her knuckles.

She put her forehead on his chest, so he ran his hands up her arms and pulled her in close. He felt her relax and take a deep breath. "Thank you for supporting me. I have to admit, I do think about what might be nice to have. I even tried to draw out some ideas, but I don't have a creative bone in my body."

"I would be more than happy to sketch you up some ideas."

"We could do that—it might be fun to see what it would look like. Do you want to come over to my place tonight? I can finally live in there now and it would be fun to cook you some dinner."

"You want to cook me dinner? I'm on board with that idea. What time? Seven? Six? In an hour?" He grinned at her.

She pushed his shoulder. "I think an hour is pushing it since it's only three. How about six thirty?"

"It's a date. I'll bring my drawing supplies."

"They aren't out in the Jeep?" She raised her eyebrows and looked at him like she was talking to an alien.

He shrugged. "My backpack is, but I'll bring a drawing board and big paper for this—so we can plan it better."

"Oh. You had me worried there for a minute."

A FEW HOURS LATER, Jeremy knocked on her door and nearly swallowed his tongue when she answered. She had on a navy blue, soft-looking dress. It had long sleeves, but was cut low in the front and the full skirt was short, hitting well above the knee. Her curves were on full display and he realized he was hungry—but not for food.

He handed her the bouquet of flowers and forced his feet to work. She took the bouquet and gave him a dazzling smile. Her lips looked like they were wet, and her eyes were all dark and mysterious. He wasn't sure he could function with her looking like she did.

"You look amazing. Are you trying to kill me?"

She laughed while he set down his drawing board and back pack. The laugh died when he pulled her into him and put his mouth on her shiny lips. She moaned and put her arms around his neck. They devoured each other—fighting for every little bit of passion, she tasted like heaven. He ran his hands over the soft dress, finding her curves underneath. She arched into him and he groaned at the contact. She smelled like flowers, and something spicy—and all woman. He couldn't get enough of her; he wanted to kiss and lick every inch of her. He wanted to worship her and possess her at the same time. But he was getting way ahead of himself—he'd come for dinner and to help her examine the idea of a reception room. So, he pulled back, to calm down and regroup.

She looked up at him through her lashes, a pretty pout on her lips. "So, how hungry are you, Jeremy?" She put her hands on his chest and ran them across the muscles. She found his nipples under his shirt and pinched them.

Oh, boy. No regrouping happening any time soon. "Starving, ravenous—but not for food."

"Perfect. Dinner will be ready in an hour or so. Do you think we can slake that other hunger in the meantime?"

Does she mean what I think she means? Dear God, he hoped so. "We can give it a good start. I'm not sure this is the kind of hunger that ever goes away. Not with you looking like you do right now." Like he wanted to rip her clothes off. "Or, well, any time, really. In fact, all you have to do is breathe and I get hungry. But maybe we could at least take the edge off."

"You might be right about that, but we can give it the old college try. Come with me, Jeremy."

"Gladly." He started walking and then stopped dead. "But I don't have any supplies for this. I didn't think we would be… Well I thought we were drawing, so I brought those supplies—but I didn't even consider…"

She laughed. "No worries. I ordered some *supplies* online the other day—just in case. They came in yesterday's mail."

"Online? Really? I never thought about buying them online."

"Stick with me, kid, and I will teach you many things."

He laughed at her old man voice, which shocked him. He had no idea he could laugh when he was so aroused. She was *already* teaching him many things.

CHAPTER
nineteen

AMBER TOOK JEREMY TO HER bedroom. He'd made her feel so protected and cherished this afternoon when they were talking about the reception idea, she just had to be with him. Maybe it was a bad idea to get involved right now—but she'd felt so lost, and he'd made her feel like they could face the world together. She needed him right now like she needed air. The whole time she was planning dinner she'd thought about how much she wanted to share her body with him. She wanted the two of them to be as close as humanly possible. She'd been so aroused by the time he actually arrived, she knew she was emanating so many pheromones he didn't have a chance.

She felt like every action she'd taken the rest of the day was in preparation for her seduction of Jeremy—not that he needed a lot of seducing. None, actually. She didn't think he'd been as wound up as she had been when he knocked on the door, but he sure hadn't put up any fight, either. And didn't that make her job easier. She smiled as she entered her bedroom. She had put clean sheets on the bed and turned them down so the mattress was ready for them. She had soft music playing and some jasmine-scented candles burning. Her bedroom window was open just enough to let in a small breath of fresh air and keep the room cool. She wanted to warm Jeremy up.

Jeremy stopped a few feet in the door and looked around. "So, this idea was not exactly spur of the moment."

"Not at all. You made me feel so special this afternoon, this is all I could think about. I did manage to put food together, but I was concentrating on getting you naked."

"I like naked."

"Good, then can we get that going?"

"Absolutely, but let's not rush. I want to savor our first time together and make it special." He crossed to her and pulled her into his arms softly kissing her. She held onto his strong shoulders and then ran her hands up and around his neck, her fingers playing with his hair. He practically purred as she caressed him.

He kissed his way to her ear and sucked the lobe into his mouth, which caused heat to curl in her belly and goosebumps to break out on her skin. He caressed her neck with his lips moving down the column to her shoulder where he nipped at the soft spot there. She squirmed against him and pulled his head back up so her hungry mouth could devour his.

He moved his hands up slowly caressing her from her waist to her breasts and fondled them. He cupped her through her dress and scanty underwear and squeezed her nipples. She arched her back to put her breasts firmly into his hands and he smiled against her mouth, with a low rumble in his throat.

She wanted more, needed more. She pressed her body to his from knees to chest and hummed her appreciation of the feel of his body against hers.

He reached behind her and found the zipper on her dress which he lowered so slowly it seemed like he was going tooth by tooth. She squirmed against him trying to speed things up, but he appeared to ignore her and continued his painstakingly slow assault on her body.

When he finally had the zipper lowered all the way he pulled the shoulders of her bodice forward and let it slip down to reveal her bra. He looked at it and gave a groan of approval.

"Very pretty—both the barely-there bra and the even prettier breasts they *almost* contain." He bent down and kissed the tops of her breasts and she felt sensation zip from his mouth straight down to between her legs. She writhed, and he held her tighter to continue his exploration. He pulled the bra down with his teeth, over her highly sensitized nipple and then moved to the other breast. She wanted his mouth on her, now. But her hands were trapped in the long sleeves and top of the dress that had pooled down around her waist. She started to free them, but he held onto her arms while he finally licked her nipple and then pulled the tight bud into between his lips to suckle her. It felt so good her knees started to melt. He backed her up so she was leaning against the dresser and then moved on to the other nipple and gave it the same treatment. She sobbed from the exquisite sensations he was flooding her body with.

"Jeremy."

"Yes, baby, we'll get there—but your breasts are so beautiful they needed my attention."

She squirmed again. "Yes, but can we do more naked."

He smiled at her. "Absolutely." She felt him reach behind her and unclasp her bra, which he took off and dropped onto the dresser. Then he pushed the dress off her hips and it fell to the floor in a silent puddle. He looked down at her tiny panties and the heels she'd put on. "*Mmm,* Now isn't that the prettiest sight I've seen in ages."

He helped her step out of the clothes and then knelt down. His mouth left little kisses on her stomach, her hips, her bellybutton and then started lower. One hand was on each of her butt cheeks as he traced her panty line with his mouth and kissed her through the lace. Her body bucked at his touch.

Finally, he dragged the drenched silk over her hips to the floor while his lips and tongue stayed busy worshipping her. She felt her bones start to liquefy and he leaned her back against the dresser and spread her legs to give his clever lips and tongue better access.

He kissed her and then licked along the seam of her sex. "You are so wet." He looked up at her with a gleam in his eye. But, the cessation of his assault allowed her wits to return.

"Yes. Can we please get you naked now? I want you— no—I need you to fill me. No more teasing, Jeremy. I want you inside now." She grabbed his hair and pulled him to his feet, yanked his shirt up out of his pants and tore at the buttons. He pulled it over his head when it was loose enough from her fumbling attempts to unbutton it. She started on his pants the second he pushed her hands aside to yank off his shirt. The belt was easy but his erection was making the zipper hard to pull down. But she was determined to do it—nothing was stopping her from getting to the prize. She managed to get the pants undone and pushed them toward the floor. His manhood poked toward her and she kissed him through his boxers. She dragged his shorts down and had both hands on him— one on his cock and the other massaging the sacks. She felt him harden and lengthen—she reveled in her feminine power over his male anatomy.

She felt him groan and grab her shoulders to pull her up. "If you don't stop that. I'm going to ruin the party before it gets started."

She smiled and rubbed her soft curves against his hard planes. It was glorious. He kicked out of his shoes and then his pants before he scooped her up and dumped her on the bed. As she bounced, he took off his shorts and socks and followed her down. She reached out and grabbed a condom from her night stand. "Suit up. Let's do this."

He laughed. "Yes ma'am." Together they managed to get the condom on. He moved on top of her and she took him in hand and guided him home. She felt him ease into her—she certainly was wet enough. She felt him stretch her and fill her.

"Amber, oh my God, you feel so wonderful—hot and wet and tight. Woman, you are amazing." And then his mouth came down on hers as he started moving. She arched up to take more of him and he slid in deeper. She was lost to the feeling of him fully inside, touching the entrance to her womb, rubbing all the sensitive places. It was exquisite.

She wrapped her legs around his waist and he slid in further. Her passion was climbing. "Faster, Jeremy. Harder."

He picked up the pace and she went higher, she felt her body gathering for release and when it erupted, she clutched him tight to her. Molten lava flowed through her veins, her muscles, her whole body. As he continued to pound into her, the orgasm went on and on—it was incredible. And when he shouted at his own release, her whole being smiled in satisfaction. He slumped on top of her, panting and sweaty. She was panting and sweaty right along with him. She reveled in his weight pressing her into the mattress. He rolled them over—to his back with her on top of him—even before she was ready to have his weight off her, but when she took a deep breath she realized he was wise to move.

"That was awesome," she said as she snuggled on top of his warm body. He was hard everywhere she was soft, and she loved it.

He ran his hands over her hair and down her back. "Yes, and you make an excellent blanket. Soft, warm skin is much better than scratchy wool or even the new fuzzy micro-fiber."

Laughing, she pushed up so she could look into his sleepy eyes. "Better than micro-fiber? Well, now. That's quite the compliment."

He grinned at her. "What can I say? I'm an author, master of words."

"Good thing you write for kids, oh mighty master of words—they love cheesy."

"Cheesy? Me? Now you asked for it." He tickled her. She squirmed on him and tried to get away, but he clamped his legs around her and held her to him.

"No fair. No tickling after sex when I'm naked and too wrung out to get away."

"I guess you're right, but you started it with your sassy mouth."

"There are other ways to keep my mouth occupied." Then she covered his mouth with hers for a long, wet kiss. "See? Like that. I told you I would teach you many things young apprentice."

He pulled her sassy mouth back down to his and she melted into the heat of the searing kiss. When they had to stop to breathe, she laid her head on his chest to listen to the pounding of his heart. When it finally slowed, she pushed up and looked him in the eye. "I believe it's now time for the meal I have prepared. Come with me—we will dine to prepare for round two."

"Round two?"

"Of course. One time will not nearly quench the hunger. Silly man." She rolled out of bed and handed him his pants and she slipped her dress back on—commando.

"And you think I'll be able to eat knowing there's nothing on under that dress?" He looked at her with flames of lust in his eyes.

She wasn't going to get caught in that gaze, so she flippantly said, "Well, I'm going to eat—even if all you can do is drool."

He growled as she ran out of the room.

CHAPTER
twenty

Jeremy went into the bathroom, threw away the condom, put on his pants, and washed his hands. What a surprise that had been—he had no idea she was planning to jump his bones the moment he walked in the door. Not that he was complaining—no sir. Not complaining. She'd obviously been anticipating it since her bedroom had been quite the scene for seduction. Before he went to eat, he was going to check on the candles she had burning around the room and put them out.

He knew she'd mentioned round two, but they might get sidetracked with the reception room planning—and they sure as hell didn't need another fire. He still wondered what she was hiding in relation to the first one, but he'd put his questions away when she needed his help. He still planned to get to the bottom of it though. He needed to clear his conscience and be confident in his trust of her.

Mouth-watering smells were emanating from the kitchen, as he walked in and he saw her shimmy as she put a salad on the table. She had some jazzy music on and she was dancing along to it. He smiled at the pretty sight she made with her messy hair and bare feet.

"What took you so long?" she asked turning toward him.

"I put the candles out so if we get busy drawing up ideas for the reception area we won't start another fire." A shadow passed across her eyes when he mentioned the fire and he knew they needed to get the air cleared.

She quickly said, "You know, I'm kind of getting a little excited about drawing up some ideas. I don't know if I'll want to implement them, but they might be fun to draw up. I can go wild with my imagination and all-out thinking of what would make a perfect place."

"Yes, you can. We can draw up whatever you want—a wish list of what would be an amazing facility."

"Goody. So, let's eat."

They ate a delicious meal of something she called enchilada pie she had cooked in a crockpot. It had a whole bunch of layers of meat and beans and tortillas. It was spicy and cheesy and had sour cream on top—it was one of the tastiest meals he'd had in a long time. While they ate, they shared their likes and dislikes on music, TV, books, and movies. He was a science fiction geek and she was a murder mystery fan. Where those two genres intersected, they had many common opinions. But since they didn't converge a lot, they moved on to talking about events in town and the mayoral race that was starting up. They both agreed the most likely mayor would be James McGregor. He was working with Nolan Thompson to replace himself as Police Chief so he could run for mayor. There were a few other people running, but none of them seemed like the right fit.

When they were nearly finished eating Jeremy said, "So give me a laundry list of what you think a wedding reception venue would need. I know you mentioned some, when Gus cornered you about it the other day, but I wasn't thinking about drawing it then."

"In the main room, there needs to be seating with tables for a couple hundred. It needs a dance floor and somewhere for either a band or DJ to set up for music. A cake and dessert table area and something that seems to be popular right now is a photo booth, although that could and probably should be in a separate room—or at least off to the side for privacy so the flashes from the photographer wouldn't disrupt the reception.

"Then, if the bride and groom wanted a buffet, rather than sit down dinner, there would need to be an area for the food. It could also be in a side area—not right in the main room. Oh, and maybe a bar area, for a cash bar-type setup. There would need to be bathrooms with multiple stalls because we don't want the entire wedding party to have to use the ones in the restaurant. And, I think there should be changing rooms so the bride could change into traveling clothes."

He interjected, "Or, they might want to hold the wedding in the room rather than at the chapel—not everyone wants a church wedding."

She frowned. "I didn't think about that."

"What about converting the storage area above to the changing rooms?"

"That might work. If it was upstairs, we would need private bathrooms up there and a much nicer staircase to walk down—now it's just a utility one. Oh, if there is anything left of it..." Her shoulders slumped. He tried to think of something to say, but before he could say anything, she shook her head and sat up straight. "And with weddings we'll need storage for the random equipment we'll eventually want to have on hand to rent. Fountains for drinks or chocolate, chafing dishes, punch bowls—stuff like that."

He breathed a sigh of relief at her determination to press on. "So, a nice room with large shelves to hold things. I noticed your current storage area could use some work to make it more efficient."

She grimaced. "That, dear Jeremy, is an understatement. It needs a *lot* of work."

"What else?"

"It would need its own entrance that was classy and beautiful and the back lot would need to be turned into a parking area—rather than just a place for trucks to unload and my employees to park. Maybe even a small garden area. The entrance would need to have room for a manned guest book and a place for gifts. I can't think of anything else, but that's quite a list already."

Jeremy stood. "Yes. So, let's put the food away and clean up. Then we can get to drawing up ideas."

THEY SPENT THE next two hours sketching four different ideas of how to arrange the space. It was so fun watching Jeremy take her ideas and get them on paper. He had a flair for adding in details and décor that made the drawings come alive. As each idea was finished she took it into the living room so it didn't influence the next one. She taped each one to the wall.

When all four of them were done, they went in to look at them side by side. She could see the potential and she would be proud to own something like he had created. But did she really have it in her to do it? And how much would it cost? Where would she find the staff she needed? Could she work with Sheila on a daily basis? Her mind was whirling with ideas and questions.

She rubbed her temples. "This is so much to think about. My brain hurts."

"Well, we could stop for a little *recreational activity*. I seem to recall you mentioning round two, and you sitting there with nothing under that dress is making me a little crazy."

"Jeremy Scott, that is a marvelous idea. Just what I need to take my mind off all this indecision." She stood up, reached behind her, unzipped the dress, and let it fall to the floor.

She heard him swallow and his eyes warmed as he looked her over from head to toe. "So beautiful."

"Thank you, but you have entirely too many clothes on."

He laughed. "My jeans?"

"Yes, your jeans. Lose them, buster."

"Right here in the living room?"

"Right here, right now." She didn't want to have to go all the way to her room and she had a nice comfy couch.

Jeremy nodded. "Well, good thing I stuck a couple of condoms in my pocket then, isn't it?"

"Ah very resourceful of you—and well prepared. Were you a Boy Scout?" she teased.

"Of course. In this town, it was a requirement. Were you a Girl Scout?"

"Where do you think I learned to cook?" She smiled in fond remembrance. "Our troop leader was the former restaurant owner, so we spent many days in the kitchen learning to cook and bake. I realized, even then, that I loved feeding people."

"But you don't do any of the cooking, do you?"

"Not too much these days. I'm too busy running the business. But, I sometimes sneak in the kitchen to indulge my love of cooking. Okay, enough of this stalling. Let's feed that other hunger that keeps popping up."

"If we must," he said with a dramatic sigh, but she could see heat in his gaze ignite as he stood and shucked off his jeans, grabbing the condoms out of his pocket.

She pushed him back down on the couch. "My turn to be on top." She straddled him, took the foil packet from him, and opened it to put it on him. Before she could get it out of the wrapper he had one hand on her clit and another on her hip holding her still. She nearly dropped the condom, it felt so good. She sighed. "Jeremy."

"It was there. It needed attention."

She grit her teeth against the pleasure and started to roll the condom down his full length, taking time to caress each inch as she went. He faulted in his ministrations on her most sensitive spot and she smiled to herself knowing she was giving him as much pleasure as he was giving her. He went back to stroking her and she felt herself getting wetter.

He leaned forward and licked her breast, then pulled the tight nipple between his lips and sucked hard. Dear God, the man was going to make her come, and he wasn't even inside her yet. She eased up and the furled bud popped out of his mouth. She positioned herself over his hard-as-steel penis and slid down on him. As soon as she had him inside, his mouth found her other breast. She rocked forward on him and he groaned as he slid deeper. The vibration against her flesh made pleasure shoot through her.

She pulled on his hair to get his face up to hers. His hands went straight to her breasts keeping up the torture as he kissed her deeply. She started moving on him, because it was either move or explode—the feelings were shredding her control. He massaged her breasts and pinched her nipples and she sucked on his tongue. He met her with a thrust each time she came down on him.

The orgasm hit her with the force of a tidal wave and swept her into a sea of bliss. He flipped her down on the couch and pumped into her. She put her legs around his back and crossed her ankles at the small of his back as she felt him stiffen. He growled her name into her neck as he came.

Neither one able or willing to move, they laid together letting their bodies calm and return to normal. Their hearts slowed, as did their breathing as their bodies cooled. She decided she could get used to this, having a man around, to stand by her and give her fantastic orgasms. But did she really want one? No, not really—maybe once in a while it would be nice, but a full-time man around?

No, she didn't like that idea too much. And she had responsibilities she didn't want anyone to know about. She didn't know when or where that responsibility would return, but it wasn't safe for him to go back up the mountain until the fire fighters were completely gone. He didn't trust anyone except her. So, she needed to distance herself from Jeremy for the time being, anyway. He'd been so amazingly helpful that she'd been overcome with gratitude—and, let's be honest, lust. But now that she'd scratched that itch, she needed to get back to being self-sufficient.

So, how to get rid of him in a nice way so he wasn't

all hurt. He was an artist, so weren't they all sensitive and soft hearted? Well she would just blame it on work. She did need to open her restaurant back up and if the paint smells were gone tomorrow she would get started building up some desserts. The ferry was bringing her supplies tomorrow; she was going to have a busy few days.

"Are you asleep?" she asked unhooking her legs from around his waist.

"No, sorry. Am I squishing you? I was just reveling in the joy of finding you." He got off her and pulled her up.

She covered herself with the lap blanket on the back of the couch.

"Are you cold? Do you want to go to the bedroom?"

"No, I just need some time to get ready for tomorrow. I'm going to have a busy day, getting the restaurant ready to open. I want to get it going again the day after. And I've taken so much of your time, I'm sure you have gotten way behind on your work. I appreciate everything you've done for me, but I don't want to get you in trouble with your publisher. So, if you need to dig in for a few days, I won't worry you are needing a pie fix." She smiled at him. Clearly, she was babbling and sounded stupid, but she wanted some distance.

He frowned. "I'm pretty much my own boss, and I work when I choose—but I can take a hint."

He got up and took his jeans to the bedroom. He came out of the kitchen a few minutes later, dressed and with his art supplies packed up.

He leaned down to give her a kiss on the cheek. "Thanks for dinner."

"Jeremy, I…"

"Don't worry, lovely lady. I'll be around. I will need a pie fix soon. Call me if you need any other drawings done." He walked out the door and didn't look back.

She'd clearly hurt his feelings and she wanted to call him back, but she didn't. She sat there feeling frozen, and a little like she'd just pushed away the best thing that had ever happened to her. But it had to be done.

She got up and took her dress to her room—she didn't want to sleep in that bed right now, with all the memories of Jeremy. So, she showered and got dressed and went down into her restaurant to work.

CHAPTER
twenty-one

JEREMY HIT HIS STEERING WHEEL as he drove away from Amber's. What the hell was that all about? The woman jumped him the minute he walked in, fed him dinner, dreamed about the new addition with him, jumped him again and then threw him out—like yesterday's garbage. He'd been lying there thinking they made a darn good pair and he'd like to spend a lot more time with her while she'd been thinking about throwing him out. Well that just went to show how much he knew about women. They were a complete mystery to him. The two of them were clearly not on the same page.

Well, fine. He didn't need her anyway. He had been putting off development of the books for the upcoming game sequel. He'd thought she was worth the extra hours he was putting in at night to work on ideas. But, maybe not—she was clearly hiding something from him about the fire and maybe he should have pushed her harder. He didn't think she was hiding anything bad like arson, but something was just not quite right. So, she clearly didn't trust him.

Well, he probably *should* dig into his work for a few days. Let her reopen the restaurant and go about her business. He could manage to feed himself. He could also get a pizza or go to Greg's bar for fried food. The Korean Bar-B-Q had a few tasty dishes, also. See he didn't need to go to her restaurant every day. Although, he *would* miss the chocolate French silk pie. Too bad. He needed to get some work done and he didn't need the heartbreak of dealing with Amber.

Wait, heartbreak? No, it can't be that—just rejection. Yeah, rejection. Not heartbreak.

He parked his Jeep and took all his stuff into his house. Laundry was another thing he'd been putting off, while spending all his time with that woman. Well, time to get his life back in order. His house was messy from just dumping things when he was home for a few minutes. And he needed to shower—he didn't want her scent on his skin.

He was just glad he'd been able to hide how hurt he was. When he'd gone to get dressed and gather his art supplies, he'd drawn her a quick sketch of the two of them. He had no idea how she'd feel about it, but he'd wanted her to have a small token of their time together. Maybe it made him a sap, but it had to be done.

Okay, time to man up and move on.

AMBER WORKED AROUND the clock getting her restaurant ready to open. She hadn't needed to, but she couldn't face her apartment—especially the bedroom with the messy bed from her time with Jeremy. Why she felt so weirded out about him, she couldn't say. So, she ignored it and worked like a fiend. When she'd been exhausted after being up for thirty-six hours, she'd finally gone up to her apartment, gotten some clean clothes out of the dryer, showered, and slept in the guest room.

After she got her restaurant open and operating again, she would deal with her room, and kitchen, and living room. All three of the rooms he'd been in.

The next morning, she opened her doors to all her regular morning customers, then her lunch crowd, and finally the dinner set. It seemed like everyone from town came in to eat or have a cup of coffee. There was only one notable exception. She'd even saved him some chocolate French silk pie, but he didn't show. Tomorrow he would, and she planned to be her normal self.

Three days later, she was getting cranky about Jeremy not showing up at her restaurant. What was wrong with him? He was one of her regulars and just because she'd sent him home, he was going to avoid her? She'd wondered if he was out of town, but she'd seen his Jeep parked out in front of Samantha's bakery this morning when she'd gone to mail some bills. No, she wasn't stalking him, just mailing bills. Yeah, except the mailman was always happy to pick up her mail from the restaurant.

She was still sleeping in her guest room and basically living in the restaurant. She hadn't gone into the kitchen or living room since he left. She knew she was being irrational but... No. No more buts. Time to quit acting like a fool. She had a lull, and she was going upstairs to deal with her home. She yelled out to her staff.

"I'll be back in a bit. Call upstairs if you need me."

Her cook called back, "Take your time, boss. No hurry, we'll be fine."

What was that all about? Had she been acting crazy around them? No. Well, maybe a little. But she was happy to have the restaurant open again, and wanted everything to be spotless and run efficiently. So, maybe she'd been a little more OCD than normal, but nothing over the top. Much.

She decided to check the kitchen first. She knew they'd cleaned up after dinner, but she probably needed to run the dishwasher. She marched into her kitchen and stopped dead in her tracks. There was a drawing on her kitchen table. Oh, God. It was of her and Jeremy, their heads together over his drawing board laughing over something he'd drawn there. She looked closer and the drawing on the board in the picture was of the two of them again, this time they were kissing, with another smaller drawing board on the floor by their feet. On that one, they were in her restaurant holding hands, surveying the work crew fixing up her restaurant. And on the hostess station at the front of the room was a stack of his kid's menus.

She sat down at her kitchen table and burst into tears. Why had she chased this amazing man away? Because she was scared to let him see the real her, that's why. Well, damn. That was a stupid reason. She'd blamed it on her secret, but she knew that was only part of the problem—the real issue was she was scared. She liked him too much, and what if he kicked her to the curb? So, she'd pushed him away instead.

"What a damn fool you are, Amber Elizabeth Clarkson."

She decided to continue to rip the bandage off her heart completely, now that she'd started. In her bedroom, she looked around at the scene of the seduction she had designed. The candles were all around, the sheets were a mess, and her clothes were strewn everywhere. She went over and picked up the pillow he'd had his head on and put it to her face to see if his scent still lingered, but it was gone. Her heart sank. It was gone just like he was.

Last, but not least, was the living room. When she got in there she saw all the drawings he'd done for her. She went over to her favorite and studied it. It was an amazing venue and she loved it. She wanted to build it and be a part of the special day where two people pledged their love to each other. She took a picture of it with her phone and emailed it to Gus at the newspaper with a short message that said, "Let's do this."

Next order of business: find Jeremy. She went into the bathroom and washed her face, then headed downstairs for pie. The mailman was just leaving, having delivered a package. It had to be the kid's menus—it was the right size and she wasn't expecting anything else. She opened the box, and there they were—and they were wonderful. She got one out, folded it, and put it in her purse. Then she got a whole chocolate French silk pie and walked to the front door. She told her hostess, Janelle, to start setting out the children's menus with the crayons that had arrived a couple days prior, and that she may or may not be back today.

"We'll be fine. Take your time. You've been working non-stop and could probably use a break." Janelle smiled at her and winked.

Shit, just what she needed. Janelle was observant and probably knew she was taking that chocolate French Silk pie to Jeremy. Well, it didn't matter because she missed him and she was going to try to get him back. She started walking to the parking area and was almost to her car when Jeremy drove in and parked behind her. He didn't even turn off the Jeep when he stormed over to her.

"I missed you and I'm not going to let you push me away." He had his hands on his hips and a firm look in his eye.

"Good, because I missed you too and was coming to tell you that. Here," she said and thrust the pie at him.

He took the pie and put it on top of her car and pulled her into his arms. She grabbed his hair and pulled his mouth down to hers. She kissed him hard and he kissed her right back. When they needed to breathe, she pulled back. "That was mean of you to avoid me."

"Yes, and it was mean of you to send me away."

Amber nodded. "Yes, it was. Let's go upstairs so I can apologize."

"Are you going to send me away after? Because, if you are, I don't want to."

She looked at him in shock. "Really?"

"Hell, no. Who am I kidding? I just won't leave quietly this time." He grabbed her hand and the pie, stopped to turn off his Jeep, and dragged her up the stairs to her rooms.

She laughed and pushed him to go faster.

CHAPTER

twenty-two

THE NEXT MORNING, SHE LEFT Jeremy passed out in her bed when she went down to open the restaurant. The new paint in the café made her smile. It looked so pretty—the blue accents made the room pop. She unlocked the front door and turned the open sign on. Kimberly, one of her waitresses, was just clocking in. She was college aged and she liked the morning shift so she could do her online classes in the afternoon. She was studying to be a Medical assistant.

"Hi, Kim. Ready for the day?"

"Yes, I am. I have a test to study for this afternoon, but I think I've got the material down pretty good—it's for anatomy." Then she burst into song. "The distal phalange is connected to the middle phalange, the middle phalange is connected to the proximal phalange, the proximal phalange is connected to the metacarpal—"

"Stop! Before you sing the entire skeletal system, I need coffee."

Kimberly laughed. "Yes, boss."

Amber got coffee and let her cook, Gary, fix her a big breakfast. She was starving from all the activity the night before. It was early enough for her to have the time to take her plate into her office to eat and check her email.

When she opened her email, she saw she had a reply from Gus about the reception venue. Apparently, she, Gus, and Jeremy had a meeting with an architect that afternoon, and he asked if she would please bring the original of Jeremy's drawing. Well, the man didn't let any grass grow under his feet—it hadn't even been twenty-four hours since she'd told him she was ready to move forward.

She thought it was a little odd that Jeremy was supposed to join them, but it was his drawing, so she didn't have a problem with it. When he managed to drag himself out of bed, and come down for breakfast, she'd let him know. Then again, Gus had CCed him on the email, so maybe he would check his phone.

There were a couple more emails in her inbox, so she dealt with them and went out to help with the breakfast rush that would be starting any minute. Her crew was ready, so she took the hostess stand for the morning.

Amber was surprised to see Janet come into the restaurant with Carrie and Gerald in tow. Janet rarely came in for breakfast, and the kids should be in school.

"Janet, it's so good to see you. Would you like some of my brand new kid's menus?"

Janet's mouth turned up in a tired smile. "That would be great, Amber. The kids have doctor's appointments later this morning—they both need shots, and since Brett is on the road, I decided to give them a treat before that."

Three-year-old Carrie piped up. "Yeah, and we can't tell Daddy because he says he's not working his fingers to the bone, when mommy can't get off her fat ass and cook. But I don't think mommy has a fat—"

Gerald grabbed her by the arm. "Look, Carrie. Some of the Tsilly books. Pick one out and I'll read it to you." He pointed to the display of Jeremy's books, but he looked cautiously around. Amber's heart broke for this seven-year-old child who was probably worried about someone hearing his sister.

Janet looked just as frightened as she looked around them, also.

Amber said, "Don't worry, just me. No one else is close enough to hear." She put her hand on Janet's arm to comfort, but Janet jerked back and winced.

She laughed shakily. "I whacked my arm on the door this morning."

Amber nodded. "Come with me." *Yeah, I'll just bet that place where she 'whacked her arm on the door' is in the shape of a hand or fist. When is she going to leave that bastard?*

After Amber seated Janet and her kids, she tried not to fume about Janet and her situation, but it was hard. She hated injustice and knew Janet's family would help her in any way they could—her mother was the mayor for goodness' sake. And Sandy and Terry would do anything for their sister. But Amber didn't know all the facts, so she needed to trust that Janet was an adult and knew what she was doing.

When Jeremy walked in the door, she almost cheered. He would distract her from Janet's plight. He had on yesterday's clothes and his hair was wet—probably from her shower. She wondered if he smelled like her jasmine-scented body wash. That idea made her smile.

"Good morning lovely lady. What puts that smile on your face this morning? Thinking about last night?"

"Actually, I was wondering if you smelled like my shower gel."

He grimaced. "Yes, in fact, I do—and it's not nearly as attractive on me as it is on you. I might have to go buy something more manly to store in your bathroom—if we are going to have more sleep-overs at your house. Can I get a table? I'm starving. You apparently, don't cook much upstairs—there was hardly enough food to feed a mouse."

"I'm not up there enough to stock a lot of food. Table or booth?"

"Yeah, you do seem to always be down here. Table—unless you're going to join me, then a booth would be better to hide any untoward activity."

"Table. There isn't going to be any untoward activity taking place in my restaurant—at least not by the owner."

Jeremy sighed and shook his head. "That is a very sad thing to hear." As he sat he said, "I don't need a menu just bring me that ginormous breakfast platter you have with a side of pancakes and coffee—lots of coffee."

"Coming right up." She turned to go, then abruptly stopped and turned back. "I almost forgot. Did you see the email about Gus setting us up in a meeting with an architect?"

"Yes, I did. And I had planned to mention it as soon as I walked in the door. But your smile and then all that talk about showering made that plan evaporate into the wind."

She smiled at his silliness. "As long as we both know about it, that's what matters."

"Yeah. How about I come by and pick you up about two fifteen? That way, you can just walk out the front door. I already grabbed the pictures we drew. I wasn't completely sure which one you chose, so I just took them all."

"That sounds fine. I'll go put in your order and get some coffee out to you." As she walked away, she asked herself if she wanted to have more sleepovers with him at her house, and did she want him to buy his own shower gel to keep in her shower. That sounded pretty intimate, and a little more committed than she was feeling.

She laughed at herself. She'd had sex with the man several times now and she was feeling intimate over shower gel? Good grief, what was wrong with her, anyway? It's just shower gel. In her bathroom. His shower gel, in her bathroom. She still felt a little freaked out about that.

And what if Owen came back while Jeremy was there? Could she trust Jeremy with her secret?

JEREMY WAS DRAGGING. He felt like he could mainline coffee and still not get enough. He'd already had one cup and was working on his second. Amber had worn him out last night and then been up early. And here he was, dragging. He'd spent the last week working like a demon on first drafts for the new sequel to the *Adventures with Tsilly* game. It wouldn't be out for another two years, but things moved slow in the publishing world, so he needed to have them ready in the next few months for editing prior to publication at release time. He decided to check the rest of his email while he waited for his breakfast.

He had a message from the game company. They'd done another focus group with the books. He sighed. Now what? But this new focus group was a little older, and they wanted graphic novels. Graphic novels? Well, at least they weren't changing the children's books—it was such a formula by now, all they really had to use the focus group for was to select which of the ten worlds in the game they wanted books for, and which adventure in that world was the best. In most games the *adventure* would be called a level, but you didn't level up in *Adventures with Tsilly*— you went on the next adventure.

But a graphic novel? This was a completely new idea. He'd always done little kids' story books. He'd never done a Tsilly graphic novel. It might be fun to try one for the Tsilly crew, but they would be a heck of a lot more work and they would need a much more involved story. A kid book was a couple dozen pages; a graphic novel was more—he didn't know exactly how long, but probably in the vicinity of a hundred pages.

The game company had included some ideas and they told him they would be doing more research into the idea. He answered them with a 'thanks for the heads up' type of email and said he would do some research into it, also. He then forwarded the whole mess to his agent, so she could start her own research. This would require a whole new contract.

Once he got his food, he probably should eat it quickly, and go home to put in some research time on what a graphic novel might entail—and he needed to read through the suggestions by the game company. Since it was a new concept he didn't know which release of the game they were looking at. The original AWT1 was put out about four years ago and then the sequel AWT2 was released last Christmas. The next sequel, AWT3, would be ready two years from this winter.

He wasn't sure he wanted to branch out into graphic novels. It might be fun to do and he might love it. But, the way the game company controlled the books was a pain in the ass—he had no room for creativity and he guessed it wouldn't be a lot different with the graphic novels.

He was still thinking about it when he finished eating and went to pay for his breakfast. He paid and told Amber he'd be back at two fifteen and left without any other conversation. He didn't even realize he'd been abrupt until he was nearly home. He hoped Amber wouldn't be offended by his distraction.

CHAPTER
twenty-three

AMBER LOOKED AT THE CLOCK AND noticed it was two fifteen. She waved to her staff and walked out the door. Jeremy was just pulling up out in front, so she went to go get in.

"Thanks. I'm sorry I was cranky when you left," she said.

At the same time, he said, "I didn't mean to be abrupt after breakfast."

They looked at each other and laughed. She said, "I didn't notice."

He shook his head. "I didn't, either. I got an email from the game company for a new idea and I was thinking about the research I needed to do on it."

"Well, that was at least a good reason for your

distraction. Mine was silly." She wasn't about to tell him she'd been freaked out about the idea of his shower gel being in her bathroom. She still thought it was a stupid thing to be freaked out about, but couldn't seem to stop herself. She could always lead him to believe it was about this meeting. Good idea. "I'm not sure what to think about this meeting with the architect."

"Probably just testing the waters and looking into options." He pulled into the parking lot at the newspaper.

"Let's do this." She jumped out of the Jeep and headed for the front door. Jeremy was right behind her with his ever-present backpack and portfolio that held his larger paper and drawing board. When they walked in, the receptionist pointed to the conference room to the right. The door was open and she heard the buzzing of voices coming from the room. They must be finishing up another meeting. She walked over to the door and peered in. Gus saw her and waved her in.

"Amber, Jeremy. Perfect timing. Let's all sit, shall we?"

Amber was shocked to see everyone that was interested in making the town a wedding destination in the room. She looked at Gus. "I thought this was with you, me, and the architect."

"Well, this here is the architect, Wes Radcliff," he said waving at a man with salt and pepper hair and a trim beard. "And I'm here and so are you, and ya came with Jeremy, so he's here, too. And I invited a few other folks so everyone would be on the same page."

"What is it with you guys and your surprise meetings?"

Barbara said, "Are you freaking kidding me? Is this another ambush? You didn't know about it *again?*"

Amber quickly shook her head. "No nothing like that. I did know about the meeting—he just didn't tell me who all was going to be here. It's no big deal Barbara. Nothing to be upset about."

"I rarely get upset about things, Amber. You know I have a cool head."

Amber worked hard not to burst out laughing. Barbara had been cool-headed before her pregnancy. But once she was pregnant, not so much. Amber just hoped that once the baby was born the cool-headed Barbara would return. She looked around the room and saw nearly everyone else had odd expressions on their faces—like they, too, were trying not to laugh. All except the architect—he clearly was from out of town. "Yes. Of course, Barbara. So, what's the plan, Gus?"

"Well, I thought we could start by showing everyone the idea you and Jeremy came up with. Then, we could open the floor to questions or concerns by the others who will essentially be vendors. If any of the discussion suggests changes needed, we can talk about that, and then at the end we can give Wes the go ahead to start designing. I've already gotten the blueprints for your building and the land plot information and given them to Wes. He can draw up the plans and then Marc can give ya an estimate on the cost to build. But, before we do that, I want to go around the table and have everyone introduce themselves to Wes, and explain why they're here at the meeting and how they'll play a role in the wedding destination."

By the time everyone was finished introducing themselves, Amber had a much better idea of how this would all work together. She hadn't reasoned it all out in her mind. Plus, she hadn't been to a wedding in several years and had never planned one, so she had no idea. This had already been an extremely informative meeting, and she was glad she'd brought paper to take notes.

She said, "So, is someone going to make up a wedding directory of everyone in this room with contact information, and an explanation of the services they offer?"

"That's a great idea, Amber. I'll get one of the new kids to work on that idea," Gus said waving toward the newsroom. "Trey will be working on the website as soon as he's released from the hotshot crew on the mountain. Although I think half the town has talked to him about websites."

Amber nodded. She knew she had talked to him about one for her place.

Gus said, "Let's get started. Jeremy and Amber, please start by going over the ideas you guys came up with for a reception hall. I printed out small copies for everyone to look at as we go along." Gus handed out a stack of papers that they passed around the table.

Amber saw Jeremy look to see which design she had picked and got it out of his portfolio. He attached it to his drawing board and then reached into his backpack and pulled out a portable easel, unfolded it, set it up, and put his drawing board on it. She grinned at him. "A portable easel? Seriously? You're kind of a geek, aren't you?"

"You're just figuring that out?" He smiled and shrugged. "I use it a lot at book signings."

"Well, geek on." She waved toward the group.

"Oh, no. This is your show—I'm just here as support."

"Fine." She turned toward the group.

For the next hour, they talked about her and Jeremy's ideas for the wedding reception venue. Several of the group assembled had questions and suggestions, but overall very little change was suggested. Primarily, the modifications were a few more access doors for deliveries and more storage of all varieties—dry, cool, cold, and frozen.

When the idea exchange wound down, Mayor Carol stood up. "This has been an excellent discussion, and it looks like we are well on the way to establishing Chedwick as a premier wedding destination. You probably all know I've been doing a lot of renovations on my home to turn it into a B&B. Fortunately, Marc is nearly finished at my place, so he'll be freed up to work on this new project. I hope we'll be able to have everything in place for next spring, so we can start having weddings. I was thinking maybe we could have a monthly meeting to check progress and try to catch any stumbling blocks before we get there. Sheila, since you'll be the wedding planner, would you please coordinate the meetings?"

"Sure, Mayor Carol. I would be happy to," Sheila said with a smile. Amber noticed Sheila seemed to be reveling in her new position and was taking it seriously. She was dressing more businesslike and took lots of notes. Amber was still amazed to see this side of her personality. What a difference a purpose and people who believed in her made. She wondered if something like that would help her secret boarder, Owen.

CHAPTER
twenty-four

JEREMY FINISHED TALKING TO THE architect. The guy seemed to have it together. He'd asked good questions during the discussion. Once that was done, Wes had asked Jeremy to spend a few more minutes in conversation. He had pointed out various things on the drawing where he wanted more explanation. Since the drawing was a bird's eye view-type of sketch, it wasn't very technical. That's what Wes would be doing—taking their ideas and creating real plans for them. They exchanged contact information for any further communication they might need.

Jeremy looked over to where Amber was sitting, staring off into space. Something was on her mind, and he wondered what it might be. He didn't think the discussion they'd just had could have gone any better, but he didn't even pretend to try to guess what she might be pondering.

Sometimes women just thought about things differently.

"So, ready to go?" he said and put his hand on her shoulder.

Amber jumped, clearly startled. "Sure, I was just contemplating something."

They walked out to his Jeep. "Want to talk about it?"

"No, I need to figure it out by myself." Her shoulders were hunched in and he wondered if it had something to do with whatever it was she was hiding about the fire. He needed to get to the bottom of that, but he hated rocking the boat.

"You know you can trust me, don't you Amber?"

"Yes, of course. But, some things are hard to explain."

"I'm a very patient listener and I will keep whatever you say in strictest confidence."

She sighed like she carried the world on her shoulders. "But, what if it's something illegal?"

"Well, how illegal are we talking? Slap on the wrist? Misdemeanor? Or felony?"

"Probably a slap on the wrist, actually, now that you put it in those terms. Maybe a fine."

"Then, it shouldn't be a big deal if you tell me." If she didn't, the curiosity was going to kill him, for certain.

She looked at her phone. "Well, maybe. I've got another hour or hour and a half before I need to get back for the dinner rush. Can we go somewhere we won't be disturbed and no one will be around to overhear?"

"My place is just down the street. Want to go there?"

"Perfect."

As he drove toward his home he tried to think if his house was a mess or straightened up. A few things were probably out, but he didn't think anything embarrassing or disgusting was visible. It should be fine, but maybe he should make a practice of keeping it neater—if he was going to have a girlfriend.

Was she a girlfriend? Or just a friend with benefits? They hadn't been out on a date. They'd spent a lot of time together, but usually it was working on projects and having sex. Nothing really *dateish*. It might be a good time to change that.

He wasn't sure when he could accomplish it—the woman worked all meal hours, from breakfast to after dinner, except for mid-afternoon and that seemed like a weird time for a date. Would some particular day be better? Maybe when the restaurant was slow, like bingo night at the grange or some service club having an event. He'd have to take a look at the paper and see what was coming up on the community calendar. Then again, he could just ask her.

"Jeremy?"

"Yeah?" He shook his head to clear his brain.

"You seem distracted. Are you feeling weird about me coming to your house?"

"No, not at all. Well, I did wonder if I had underwear lying around or science experiments in the sink, but I think I'm okay on both fronts."

She laughed. "I have a brother, so I don't think you can scare me easily."

"Yes, but I imagine Barbara doesn't let him get away with much."

"You're probably right about that. They have been married forever—right out of high school. And Mom always tried to keep him in line before that."

"I can't even imagine getting married at that age, can you?" he asked.

"No, not really. I had a boyfriend in high school and dreamed about it, as all girls do, but once we graduated and he went off to college that was pretty much the end of that. And believe me, that is a good thing—he came back a year or so ago, and I am so glad we drifted apart. He was kind of a jerk. Acting like I was somehow beneath him because I was still at the restaurant. It didn't seem to matter to him that I was the owner, rather than a waitress. Jerk."

"Yeah sounds like you are better off without him." Jeremy was surprised at the surge of jealousy he felt when she talked about her old boyfriend. It didn't seem terribly rational to feel that way for a friend—guess he'd turned the corner to girlfriend. He wondered if he was alone in that or if she was with him.

He was glad to turn into the driveway at his house. He needed a different thought pattern and hopefully she was going to tell him her secret. That should get his mind focused elsewhere. He grabbed his portfolio and backpack out of the backseat and walked with her up his sidewalk.

What would she think of his place? He had always been happy there and was satisfied with the way things looked, but what would she think? She'd been there before—at night—but, this time he was walking in with her in the daylight. Seeing it through her eyes, he noticed things he normally ignored. The flower-beds were over-run with weeds. He hadn't planted them, so he didn't take a lot of time on them. He weeded them early in the spring and summer, but once it started toward fall, he didn't pay much attention. The book tour he'd been on was a convenient excuse for ignoring them, but it had very little to do with that and more to do with there not being many flowers this time of year, so why bother?

Amber didn't seem to even be looking at his yard. She seemed preoccupied—maybe she was worrying about what she was going to tell him. Yeah, that was probably it He was getting all freaked out for nothing. He unlocked the door and ushered her into his living room. It looked fine—he had comfortable furniture, a huge TV and there was a fireplace because it got darn cold at the foot of the Cascade mountains in the winter. They didn't get much snow—but it got cold, and the breeze off the lake didn't help with that. Nearly everyone had a fireplace and a huge pile of wood ready to burn.

"Do you want something to drink? I have soda and juice. I could make coffee. Or I have a beer or two, I think."

"Maybe just a glass of water, unless you can whip up a margarita."

"No, not so much." He raised his eyebrows wondering if she was serious.

"I was just kidding, anyway. Liquid courage and all that."

"No need for courage—liquid or otherwise. It's just the two of us having a friendly talk." He hoped it wasn't something really bad since he didn't want to have to rat her out, but there were some things he couldn't ignore as a firefighter.

AMBER FORCED HERSELF to smile, he was trying to be supportive, but it wasn't helping. She didn't know if she should be telling him this or not. But she was tired of hiding it and she could use a second opinion.

He waved to the living room. "Have a seat and I'll get you some water."

She sat on the couch. Well, sat might be a stretch—she perched on it. It was comfortable enough, but it just didn't seem like the right place for this talk. She got up and followed him into the kitchen. He walked out and nearly mowed her down.

"Are you alright? I nearly crashed into you."

"I'm fine. Can we sit at the table?"

He backed into the kitchen and set her glass down. "Sure, let me move the papers and crap off of it. I use it for more of a workspace than for meals."

"That's because you never eat at home."

"I do sometimes—not often, but sometimes."

"Don't you have an office? The house seems big enough for one."

"Yeah, I do—but the light is better in here." He shrugged.

"A true artist—it's all about the light." She noticed he winced at her statement and she wondered what that was about. A shadow seemed to pass through his eyes, but it was gone too quick to understand it. Maybe she hadn't really seen it at all.

He gathered up papers, pencils, erasers, a pencil sharpener, and felt tip pens. There were drawings. Some were just sketches, others were ink outlines, and some were completed drawings that could easily fit into a book. Some had dialogue or narration and some were just pictures. It was fascinating to see all the different aspects in one big pile. She also saw what looked like legal documents and some others that looked like a script. She would ask him all about it. Someday—but not today. Today was for a different discussion.

Once he'd moved everything to one end, he motioned to the table. "Have a seat. You should be safe from the paper monster, now."

She laughed as she was supposed to. He sat across from her and handed her the glass of ice water he'd made. She took a big drink and set it down. Folding her hands in front of her on the table she took a deep breath.

"It all started a few months ago—when the forest fire got bad up on the mountain. I'm sure you've heard all about Ted and how he came to be displaced."

Jeremy nodded.

"Well, at first, I thought it was all the same issue, I had some things missing from the restaurant and the back area. The trash was disturbed several times. I would go out to put some new trash out and the bags would be opened and food would be missing. I know that sounds gross, but in fact we keep throwaway food separate from real garbage. We can't keep and sell it past the expiration time, so we bag it up and throw it away—but if a person was desperate, they could eat it and not do any harm to themselves."

"Okay, so it was—or wasn't—Ted?"

"Well some things were. But after Ted was taken into custody and then returned to his family, the activity continued. So, I started to wonder if the fire had displaced someone else. There is a lot of land up in those mountains. I thought it was entirely possible that more than one person was living up there, off the land."

"Yeah, I could see that. So, what did you do?" he asked.

"I just waited in the dark one night to see what would happen. It seemed to me the trash was disturbed every third night. So, I took my pepper spray—just in case—and I waited in a dark corner to see who was disturbing my trash."

He frowned. "Pepper spray? Seriously? That was a very dangerous thing to do. It gives me chills to think about it."

She rolled her eyes at his attitude. "Oh, come on Jeremy. We live in a quiet, peaceful town."

"Yeah. Where we were having a string of burglaries."

"This was after Ted was caught."

"Yeah, and you were still having theft problems." He folded his arms and was still frowning.

"So, are you going to nag or listen?" she said frowning back at him and crossing her arms.

He ran his hands through his hair making it stick up at funny angles. Then he sighed and said, "I'll listen, but I might lecture more later. I reserve the right to lecture."

"Fine. By the time the story is all told you'll probably have more things to complain about, anyway."

He groaned.

"Anyway, I waited in the dark with my pepper spray and some take out cartons of food left over from that night. About three in the morning, I saw a movement and just sat still as stone to see what was happening. A tiny pen light came on directed into the dumpster. I saw an older man looking through the bags. He had on what looked like army fatigues and a ball cap on backward."

"A vet?"

"That was my guess. I very quietly said, 'I have some fresh food here if you want some.' He went perfectly still, so still I had trouble seeing him. But I just repeated myself and added that I meant him no harm. He took the bag he was using for storage and walked slowly to where I was sitting." She thought back to that night and realized she had never felt any fear around him.

She continued, "He said 'You want to give me food?' and I said, 'Yes I do.' He took off his hat and bowed to me and said, 'Well, I kindly accept and I appreciate your generosity." He took the food I had for him and disappeared into the night.

"The next morning, on my car, there was a handful of wildflowers in the windshield wipers." She smiled at his sweet gesture of thanks. "So, I started waiting for him every third night and gave him enough food for three days. Eventually, he would talk to me for a few minutes before he disappeared. I found out he was indeed a vet named Owen and the fire and the sounds it made caused him to have flashbacks, so he was staying off the mountain until the guys put it out."

She shook her head. "He didn't have a high opinion of himself, and said he was just a loser who needed to stay away from good people. I tried to convince him otherwise, and hoped to get him to talk to someone about his situation—to see if he could get real help—but he refused." She took a deep breath and continued on.

"When it started getting colder out, I worried about him and eventually coaxed him into staying in my banquet room. I got him a space heater and a cot. I had also found out by then that he loved corn chips, so I often gave him some as a treat. And that's how the fire really got started. I'm sure it was an accident and it probably scared him. I haven't seen him since." Her throat was thick and she realized she was very worried about her friend.

CHAPTER
twenty-five

JEREMY TOOK HER HANDS AND rubbed his thumbs over the back of her knuckles. He was shocked at what she revealed, but he was determined to help her. His mind whirled with thoughts. What if someone else in town knew him? They were in a pretty remote area for someone to pick to live. Maybe he had connections in town. Owen wasn't a very common name. Could it be short for something?

"I'll help you find him—he's probably fine and just worried you're mad at him."

"I'm not mad at him." She shook her head.

Of course not—he'd yet to see her get mad about anything. "I know that, but if he's down on himself he might think you are, too. Did he tell you his last name? Or was it on his fatigues?"

She shook her head and then nodded. "There was a name on his fatigues—it was Hoyt."

"Any guess how old he is?"

"Maybe ten years older than we are? Maybe fifteen?"

Jeremy thought about that fifteen years was too far apart for him to know anything. Even ten years would be pushing it—a second grader and a senior. Unless he was really outgoing or some kind of a star athlete. Bummer. But, not about to give up, he did some quick thinking about who might be that age. "Fifteen years older than us, would put him at Hank Jefferson's age. If he went to school here, Hank might know him. I can't think of any Hoyts living in the area, but we might be able to check records and see if some lived here before."

"How will that help find him?" she asked.

"Well, if he lived here it might give us an idea of what part of town to look in. If someone knew him, they could know his interests or habits. It's a small town and a small school—when I went there we knew nearly everyone from first grade to the high school seniors."

Amber nodded. "That's true. I didn't know everyone well, but I could recognize them or their name. With less than two hundred students it wasn't hard."

"Exactly. So, for instance, if I was Owen, what would you know about me to tell someone looking for me?" He was curious about what she remembered about him.

"That you have a sweet tooth, and to check out the bakery area, or anywhere with pie." Her eyes twinkled with mirth.

He tugged on her hair. "You only figured that out recently. I kept my sweet tooth secret."

"Not completely. I knew you loved the chocolate French silk pie—I just didn't know you also ate cinnamon rolls and brownies. But, Samantha would have known those pieces."

"True, so several resources would be better. Mrs. Erickson might be the best—not only did she teach every one of us, but she also remembers everything. She might forget to take cookies out of the oven, but everything about any one of us is crystal clear. Sometimes it's more than I wish she remembered." He'd heard some of the stories she told about his fellow firefighters when they had gone by to check on her. He was terrified about what she might remember about him.

"Yeah, I hear you on that, but let's see," she said tapping one finger to her mouth. "If you were asking me about yourself, from what I remembered from high school. I would say your art, naturally. And, if I recall, you liked to play basketball, and fish in a stream, not the lake."

"Perfect. That's exactly what I had in mind, so if you were looking for me you would go to either of the streams—because clearly, I would be happy to catch fish for my dinner. But which stream would I most likely be at based on where I lived?"

"The one to the north-west," she said decisively.

"Correct, because it's closer to my house growing up, so it would be more familiar territory for me. Let's see if we can find out if Owen lived in the area. And if he did, if we can find anyone to give us some inside information."

"I wonder if he has family somewhere who is worried about him?"

"Possibly. There's probably lots of things we can look into." Jeremy grabbed a pen and piece of paper and started making notes. "Okay. We start with high school and town records, see if he's from here. If yes, then we find out which class he was in, and ask some questions. For sure we talk to Mrs. Erickson, and then anyone who was in school at the same time—let's go five years older and five years younger.

"If he's not from Chedwick, then we start expanding our search to the neighboring towns in the Chelan valley, then Wenatchee and growing larger until we get a hit. We could also see if we can get any info from the Army or Navy, what color were the fatigues?"

She frowned. "Color? What does that matter?"

"Different forces have different colors of combat uniforms. I'll grab my laptop and you can show me which ones they look like."

She decided that they might be the Air Force fatigues. She said they were faded and not very clean, so it was hard to tell—but that was her best guess.

Jeremy decided he would do some investigation while Amber was at work. He decided to start with his laptop to see what he could dig up on a person named Owen Hoyt. He put that name in a search engine and found some results—a few on Facebook and Twitter and LinkedIn. He started by reading up on those and quickly dismissed them. One was thirty-four, too young, and another was serving in the armed forces currently. None of them fit what Amber had said.

So, he started looking for references to that name in the Chelan valley. He did a search for property and didn't find anything for anyone with the last name of Hoyt. Well, that was disappointing. He'd pretty much decided the guy was hanging around because he'd lived here. But he didn't give up right away and decided to try the newspaper. No Hoyt in the newspaper, but he did get hits on an Owen Nelson, who had been one of the kids on the high school baseball team. And it would have been about the correct timeframe. Hank Jefferson had been on the same team. Well, now. Isn't that handy.

He tried Hank's cell phone, but it went straight to voicemail. He left a voicemail asking Hank to call him. Some of the areas on Hank's ranch did not have good cell reception, so he tried the ranch phone and it also went straight to voicemail. He decided one message was enough. But, he had one more number to try, so he called the house phone.

"Jefferson residence, Beth speaking."

"Hi Beth. This is Jeremy Scott."

Beth squealed in his ear. "Really? I just love your books. Do you have any new ones coming out? Can you write one about a really brave little girl with blond hair and blue eyes, named Beth, that goes on a really amazing adventure to New Zealand? We learned all about New Zealand today in school and it sounds like a really fun place to go visit. Although they do have really big eels like as big as my daddy and that might be kind of scary to see, but I'm sure the really brave little girl in your book wouldn't be afraid at all." She took a breath and Jeremy saw his chance.

"That's a great idea Beth I'll ask my publisher. But, right now, I'm looking for your dad. Is he home?"

"Nope, he's out on his horse with mommy and I am watching my brothers. It's a really important job—five year olds can be so demanding and twins make it even worse. Vance, Lance, you stop that right now. I'm sorry, Mr. Scott, I have to go. They are going to kill each other. Thanks for calling and think about that book. Boys ,I told you to stop it right no. I am going to go call Mike if you don't—"

The line went dead and he hoped Mike wasn't too far away. He was also glad he'd left a message on Hank's cell phone, because he was pretty certain Beth wouldn't be telling her father he even called. Man, six kids had to be a handful, of course the three older ones were nearly grown with Alyssa in her final year at high school and the boys were older than Alyssa. Ellen had been a brave woman taking on those three and then having three more of her own. Then again, she was a third-grade teacher when they got married so she was used to a crowd.

And that reminded him of his third-grade teacher, Mrs. Erickson, whose retirement had brought Ellen to town in the first place. He flipped through his phone and found her contact number.

"Hello, is this Jeremy? That's what my phone says."

"Yes, Mrs. Erickson. This is Jeremy Scott. I was

wondering if you had a few minutes to chat with me. I have some questions."

"Yes, I do. I'll see you here in ten minutes. I'll start the tea."

The line went dead and Jeremy shook his head. Guess he was having tea, and normally that meant cookies, too. Which, since the fire department had convinced her to stop baking her own before she burned down her house, would be from Samantha's and he loved Samantha's baking. He got his backpack with the notebook he'd been using to record all his findings and headed out to his Jeep.

Jeremy pulled up to Mrs. Erickson's house and grabbed his backpack. As he walked up the steps on the porch he noticed evidence of repairs, there were a couple of new boards that didn't have the weathered look like the rest. Clearly, someone had been by to help her out, he was glad to see it because he would never be able to do something like that. He could draw anything but hammer and nails were not his friend, or saws or screwdrivers. He'd tried using some of those tools over the years and let's just say, he needed to leave those occupations to others. He'd built a clock once in high school wood shop, and not one angle was square. He'd stuck to art classes as electives after that fiasco. He was sure the shop teacher breathed a sigh of relief when he didn't sign up again.

Mrs. Erickson opened the door. "What are you doing, Jeremy? You've been standing in that same spot forever."

"Just reminiscing. How are you today, Mrs. Erickson?"

She huffed. "Well, I'm growing old waiting for you to

get in here for tea. If you don't get a move on it's going to be cold and I'll have to start over."

"Yes ma'am," he said as he hustled in the door. If she started over, he would be there forever. "You didn't have to go to all that fuss just for me."

"Oh, you hush now, Jeremy. I'm a polite hostess and always offer my guests tea."

As she bustled around making him tea and a plate of cookies, he got the notebook and a pen out of his backpack. Setting it in his lap he took the cup and plate she handed him and had a nice sip of tea and a bite of cookie before continuing the conversation.

"Thank you, Mrs. Erickson, that does hit the spot. So, as I told you on the phone, I have some questions. I was wondering about Owen Nelson."

"Owen Nelson? He was a good boy. Kind of quiet and reserved, like you were. And he liked to draw, too. He always drew airplanes." She crossed her arms and frowned. "The boy had trouble reading though and it vexed him. I tried and tried to help him but he said the letters moved on him. We know now, that is Dyslexia, but back then…"

She sighed and shook her head. "When he fell behind the other students in school he got quieter and more withdrawn. Some children act out when they have trouble in school and become bullies or the class clown. I could name a few that gave me trouble… But I won't, because it wouldn't be professional of me." She sat back looking fierce.

What should he say to get back on track? He couldn't

imagine trying to corral a whole room full of eight-year-olds—let alone teach them anything.

Mrs. Erickson drew in a breath and continued speaking. "But Owen? He was a good boy. He lived in one of those larger houses over by where Greg's family lived. Don't get me started on Greg—that boy is smart as a whip, and why he's not using that brain for something besides running a bar is beyond me. Why in my day—"

Jeremy cleared his throat to interrupt her tangent on Greg. He thought almost everyone wondered why Greg had left law school to come back and run the bar. "Yes, ma'am. I have a few more questions about Owen."

"Well, don't just sit there, boy. Ask them."

So, he did and she answered as best she could. He scribbled notes, munched on cookies, and steered her back to the topic when she started off on a bunny trail. Especially the embarrassing ones about himself. He managed to get all his questions answered and only drank one and a half cups of tea and ate a few cookies. He thanked her profusely and escaped, before he turned into a walking tea-cup.

As he was leaving Mrs. Erickson's house he got a call back from Hank Jefferson.

"Hi, Hank. Thanks for calling me back."

"I had to. I've been hearing about you calling the house for the last fifteen minutes. I don't care why you're calling. You must come to dinner tonight, so I can get Beth to calm down. If you do me this huge favor, after dinner we'll go lock ourselves in the barn, or somewhere away from her, and we can move on to your agenda."

Jeremy laughed out loud. "I did talk to your Beth and I understand completely. I will come for dinner. See you in a few minutes."

"Thank God. You are now my favorite person."

After a crazy dinner with Beth and the family, in which Jeremy kind of promised to put Beth in a story. as soon as he could manage it, Jeremy and Hank did indeed lock themselves in the barn.

Hank said, "So, I bet you wished you had cut off your fingers before you called me, don't you?"

Jeremy laughed. "She's a sweet heart. A little high strung, but a good girl."

"Never said she wasn't a good girl, but I'm getting kind of old to handle all the enthusiasm, for lack of a better word. I'm glad Alyssa tries to reign her in, some. Since she was nearly the same at that age, she owes me—and Beth looks up to her big sister. So, why did you call me?"

"I wanted to ask you about Owen Nelson."

A shadow passed over Hank's features. "That's a name I haven't heard in years. He was a good guy. Went to high school with him, played baseball together. We were friends, but not real tight—well not until we were seniors in high school, anyway. That all changed one day."

"What happened?"

"Well, the darndest thing. Owen was always talking about joining the Air Force during our senior year of high school. He'd talked to some guys that came to town to recruit kids. Mostly the Army and Marines, but one day an Air Force recruiter came, so Owen went to the recruiting office during lunch to officially sign up. When he got back to school, Owen was acting really strange. He just sat in class with a glazed expression on his face. When class was over, he still just sat in his chair staring straight ahead.

"So, I went over to him and nudged his shoulder and said, 'Hey buddy time to go home.' Owen looks up at me with a vacant stare like he couldn't process. So, I tugged on his shirt and told him to come out to my truck and we can talk. He followed me and climbed in the truck.

"Once we were in I asked, 'So what's up dude?' Owen looks at me and said, 'I'm not Owen Nelson.' I said, 'Sure you are, who else would you be?' He said, 'I'm Owen Hoyt.' I said, 'What?' He said, 'My mom remarried Alex Nelson when I was just a little kid, maybe three. When she enrolled me in school she enrolled me as Owen Nelson. So, for my whole life I've been Owen Nelson. But today I found out that I'm not Owen Nelson, I'm Owen Hoyt. Alex never adopted me and they never changed my name legally to Owen Nelson. My legal name is Owen Hoyt.'"

Hank shrugged. "I told him that really sucked and from that day on, he considered me his best friend. He never mentioned his real name to anyone and he even graduated as Owen Nelson, but when he went into the Air Force, it was as Owen Hoyt."

"That's a very strange story, but it does explain some things." Jeremy went on to tell Hank about what had happened at Amber's. Hank was quiet and staring off into space when Jeremy finished his tale, so he waited in silence for Hank to finish his thoughts.

Finally, Hank nodded decisively and looked at Jeremy. "I'm damn glad to hear he's still alive even if he is living off the grid. I would be happy to help you look for him—we can take the horses or four wheelers into the mountains if we need to. If we find him and he still wants to live off the grid, he can stay in one of my outbuildings. I've got a couple of cabins farther out on the range for shelter from storms, if we get caught out there. They're nothing special, but better than a cot in Amber's meeting room. And if he wants to, he can always sign on as a hand. I can always use more help, especially now that the meat demand in town has risen, due to more tourists. On top of that, my older kids are making noise about college. Especially Alyssa— she's hellbent on attending Colorado State University for their veterinarian school. I hate the idea of her being so far from home, but it's ranked the third best veterinary school in the U.S. and the others are even farther away. I was hoping she would just go to WSU, they've got a veterinary program. But, no. It's got to be Colorado for that one."

"She's always liked animals so that makes sense and Colorado is what? A two-day drive? Not too far, Dad. I like your idea about Owen using one of your cabins or signing on as a hand. So, what can you tell me about his growing up? Maybe, we can get enough hints to track him down."

They talked a while longer about where Owen had lived and what he enjoyed doing. Jeremy took notes and asked questions and Hank answered with whatever he knew. It wasn't a lot to go on, but Jeremy knew every little bit would help.

CHAPTER
twenty-six

JEREMY DIDN'T COME IN FOR DINNER and Amber tried not to be disappointed. She knew it was silly, they'd just spent the whole afternoon together, but she was down. She tried to tell herself it was nerves about telling him about Owen, but she knew it had nothing to do with that. Jeremy was trustworthy, and he wouldn't want to cause the old guy harm, anyway. So, why was she feeling sad that he hadn't come by? She couldn't be missing him, could she? They'd only been spending time together for a few weeks. She couldn't be that involved already. No that was just crazy thoughts. Wasn't it? Well, she wasn't going to think about it, and she was *not* going to be all pouty that he wasn't there.

And then, he walked in the door and she felt a big

smile form on her face. Well, for goodness sake, she'd clearly lost her mind, but her feet started walking toward him—whether her mind was on board or not.

"I have one piece of chocolate French silk pie left. Do you want it?"

"God no, I am stuffed to the gills with food. Gobs and gobs of food. I may not eat for a week." He groaned as he flopped into a chair.

"Then why did you come to my restaurant, if you don't want food?"

He looked at her like she had two heads. "Well, to see you, silly girl. That's why I come most of the time to your restaurant. I just eat so I don't look like a stalker."

"No. That's ridiculous, you've been eating here for years. I've worked here since I was sixteen and I can't ever remember a time you didn't come in."

"Yeah, I started eating here the day you started working here. Well at least as soon as I found out you were working here—I might have missed it by a few days. I always thought you were so pretty, but knew I was too much of a geek to have you notice me. Well that, and I'm four years older than you."

She was flabbergasted, he couldn't possibly have been coming in to see her. "Nine years? Nine years you've been eating here? To see me? In nine years, you couldn't work up the courage to ask me out? That's the stupidest thing I've ever heard." She felt like punching him in the nose.

"In case you haven't noticed, I still haven't asked you

out. We've worked together and slept together, but we've never been on a real date."

She put her hands on her hips. "Well, I think it's about time you pulled up your big boy panties and manned up."

"I would love to take you out, Amber. Will you go out with me?"

The man was an idiot—she had to command him to ask her out. Well, she wasn't going to make it easy for him. "Thanks for asking, Jeremy. I'll think about it." She turned on her heel and started walking.

He growled. "Oh, no you don't." He jumped out of the chair, grabbed her by the arm, and spun her around. She was laughing when he put his mouth on hers and bent her over his arm and kissed the stuffing out of her.

She kissed him right back, running her hands through his hair and holding on tight.

He pulled back a little and said, "Say yes."

"I think I need to think some more."

He kissed her again even more ardently than before, then pulled back and said, "Say yes."

"Well, maybe."

And he kissed her again, so hot and furiously she thought the overhead sprinklers might come on. He pulled back again and said, "Say yes."

"Yes, Jeremy. I'll go out with you on a real date. Just as soon as we can figure out a time."

He groaned and stood her back up on her two feet. "Woman, you just might be the death of me."

"Nah, I think you can handle it. So, do you want to go

upstairs and make out?" she purred, trying to sound sexy.

"That would be awesome, but I need to tell you of all my accomplishments."

She blinked. "What kind of accomplishments?"

"Investigative accomplishments."

"That sounds interesting." She raised her eyebrows as he stood there grinning. He reminded her of a little kid who had done something in secret that he was very proud of.

"Oh, it is. Very much so."

"Well, let me tell the staff I'm leaving—so they can close up, and we can go upstairs and you can tell me all about it. Then, afterward, we can make out."

"That sounds like a perfect plan."

A few minutes later they were climbing the stairs to Amber's apartment. She took his jacket and hung it on the coat rack then she kicked off her shoes and led the way into the living room. "Let's snuggle on the couch and you can tell me about all your fun activities this afternoon. While I was slaving away at work."

"I'm not sure I would classify them as fun. Informative, yes. Fun? The jury's still out on that. Anyway, I went home and got online after dropping you off here. I looked up Owen Hoyt. I got a few hits, but none of them matched your description. So, then I tried just Owen here in the Chelan Valley, and I found some newspaper articles for an Owen Nelson, who was on the high school baseball team at about the right time."

"But why would he have a different name?"

"That's the second part of the story and you are going to have to hear it in order, young lady." He tapped her on the nose.

She crossed her arms. "Fine, continue."

"So, next I called Mrs. Erickson and she didn't even let me tell her what I wanted. She just said she would put the tea kettle on and see me in a few minutes, and hung up the phone."

Amber laughed at him. Mrs. Erickson was famous for her tea and cookies. "Well, that sounds just like her. So, did you drink tea and eat cookies?"

"Yes, I did. Samantha's cookies. They were of foreign landmarks so I ate an Eifel Tower and a Tower Bridge."

"Better than eating a Tsilly cookie—the really disturbing ones are Kalar. It just seems wrong to eat Kalar." She shuddered. Eating cookies shaped like people seemed cannibalistic to her.

"True, but Samantha once told me they are her best sellers, so not everyone feels weird about eating a strong warrior woman or a lake monster. Anyway, I asked Mrs. Erickson about Owen Nelson. She remembered him, naturally. He used to have trouble reading—she thinks now that he had dyslexia, but back then not as much was known about it, so they just marked the kids as being poor readers. She lamented about the lack of knowledge, about things like dyslexia and ADHD, during most of her forty-seven years of teaching."

"That would be hard, wouldn't it, to find out years later that your difficult students really had a learning disability.

Wishing you could go back in time with the knowledge available now and help those students. Doctors probably feel that way, too. I never thought about things like that." She shook her head and decided she was glad all she had to do was feed people.

"Yeah, I wonder how much of Owen's feeling of low self-worth you mentioned has to do with his dyslexia."

She gasped at that statement. That would explain so much. "Good question, there are probably a lot of people running around with low self-esteem that is based on false 'facts'. Probably a lot more than anyone would ever guess."

Jeremy shifted in his seat, tugged on his shirt, and cleared his throat. "Anyway, she went on to say that Owen had always had a thing for airplanes, and drew them a lot. Drawing the planes seemed to help calm him, when he was feeling agitated, so she never stopped him from doing so."

"And we think he was in the Air Force. That makes sense, but what about the last name thing?"

"Well that brings me to my second interview."

"But wait, what embarrassing thing did Mrs. Erickson remind you about?"

"Nothing," he said as his ears turned red.

"Liar. Come on, out with it."

THE LAST THING he wanted to do was tell her what Mrs. Erickson had mentioned. It was right up there in the top ten most embarrassing moments in his life and of course, a woman with a steel trap mind would have to be the one to observe it.

"It was on the playground, where nearly all embarrassing moments take place—at least for me. I was on the climbing dome trying to impress a girl. I can't even remember who it was now. Sandy, Samantha—hell it could have been Barbara, I don't remember. Anyway, I kept going higher but was starting to get a little uncomfortable. I wasn't the most athletic kid back then. Well, I'd gotten out of my climbing comfort zone and one hand slipped so I panicked. My feet started sliding in opposite directions of each other and I was trying to grab onto the bars before I fell. My pants were a little too tight and they split open giving the whole class a view of my Spiderman underwear. Everyone started laughing and I got so flustered trying to hide my underwear that I fell off the monkey bars and broke my arm. I had to go to the clinic to get my arm set in my split pants. It was not a fun day."

He looked at Amber's face and could tell she was trying to hold back. "Go ahead and laugh." His face heated with embarrassment.

She shook her head. "No, you had enough laughing that day. I'm sorry it was traumatic for you," she said with just a slight chuckle.

"Thanks, it was traumatic for an eight-year-old in

the throes of first love." He sighed dramatically trying to remember which girl it was he'd had the crush on.

"With a girl you can't even remember."

"Yes, but it was important then. In fact, maybe I blocked it out because of the pain it caused—not to my heart as much as my arm and self-esteem. But all the kids drew on my cast and that was cool. All the girls put hearts by their names and then the other boys were jealous."

"Ah, a lady killer even back then."

He snorted. "Right. So, before I called Mrs. Erickson, I called Hank's house phone and got Beth."

Amber laughed. "Oh, she's quite the handful. Hank brings her in for daughter-daddy-date night like he did with Alyssa and it's nearly like déjà vu."

He told her all about his conversation with the eight-year-old and then Hank's phone call, and by the time he got through telling about dinner, she was laughing so hard she had to get up and run to the bathroom.

She came back from the bathroom still chuckling. "You know that this is Hank's fault. Alyssa was just as precocious at eight as Beth is. He's the common factor, with the girls coming from two different mothers, so it must run in his blood," she said with a snicker.

"I did not point that out to him." He valued his life, after all, and wasn't stupid.

"No, I wouldn't either. So, moving on past Beth, what did Hank have to say about Owen?"

"Oh, that's where it gets interesting." Jeremy told her

about how Owen found out about his real name, and how he had confided in Hank only.

"Well, that could certainly add to his feeling of displacement. No wonder he lives in the woods and doesn't want to interact with people. Does his mother and stepfather still live in town?"

"No, Hank said they moved a few years after Owen graduated from high school." Jeremy had lost his parents shortly after high school in a car accident, so he knew how it would feel for Owen to come back and have them gone.

She sighed. "Well, that just sucks. He might have kept in touch with them, but he doesn't feel like he belongs to their family. So, he lives here where he feels more comfortable. Has Hank seen him?"

"He said now that we mentioned it, there was a guy he saw at a distance a few times that looked vaguely familiar. But he never approached him."

"So even his 'best friend' wasn't available." Her eyes were huge and kind of glassy looking.

He rushed on to the good news, hoping to keep her from crying. "Hank would like to rectify that and he'd like to help in any way he can. He even said he would be happy to go out on a search party. He says he would have no qualms making him a ranch hand, if he wanted, or just give him a place to bunk. Apparently, there are some outbuildings on his ranch they use in emergencies, but he said Owen could have one on a permanent basis if we can find him."

She sighed and blinked a couple of times. "That's really

nice of Hank. Did he have any other ideas of where to look?"

"Yeah, he gave me some more clues. I think I'll go into City Hall tomorrow and see if we can get a detailed map of the surrounding area, then try to put some of these clues together, and find some places to search."

She nodded. "It might be a good idea to get Trey down here to ask what they found up there during the forest fire. They might have found a second burned out cabin. Or they could at least tell us where they've been recently that Owen would have avoided."

"Good idea. You never know what they found up there tramping around all those mountains."

"So, do you want to make out now, or do you have more investigations that you did today?"

He chuckled. "I have no further reports to give, so I am free to make out, if that is what you would like to do with the rest of the evening. Although, we do need to talk about finding time for a date."

"I really appreciate all the time you spent today trying to find out about Owen. I didn't have any ideas on how to help him other than giving him a place to crash at night, in out of the cold. But you've found out so much about him and even have him a real place to stay, if we can find him. You're a pretty darn special man, you know that, right?"

"Just trying to help."

She stood up and climbed onto his lap, straddling him. "I know and I appreciate it—more than you can know. So, how would you feel about making love to celebrate all your hard work today?"

"I wouldn't be opposed to that idea, but you don't owe me anything, either. I didn't do it to curry favors. I did it to help a fellow human being who is down on his luck." He didn't want her to feel obligated to be with him.

"And that makes it even better." She ran her hands through his hair and tilted his face up to hers, so she could kiss him. She swept her lips back and forth on his, softly. Then she pressed in, to cover his mouth with hers and licked his bottom lip. He opened to her, and she swept her tongue in. She tasted like sin. It was delicious. Their tongues danced.

The fire between them built little by little. Each touch, each caress, kindling the flame. Each lick, each kiss, adding fuel. Each breath, each whisper, fanning the blaze; until it was an inferno of raging passion. There was no outside world—there was nothing except the two of them caught in a maelstrom of desire.

He wrapped his arms around her lifting her. He stood and carried her to the bedroom. She wrapped her legs around his waist, her hot center pressed against his erection. Thankfully, her bedroom was close—he wasn't sure he could have gotten them much farther.

He sat on the bed then leaned back to pull her polo shirt over her head. She had a sports bra on underneath and he was surprised at the flare of desire he felt seeing her hard nipples poking out toward him through the soft material. He'd never thought of a sports bra as sexy, but on Amber, it was.

She tore at his shirt, pulling it out of the waistband of his jeans. He helped her free it and pulled it over his head. When she ran her hands up his chest he groaned in pleasure. He pulled her sports bra off and threw it to the side. Both his hands were on her breasts, weighing them, squeezing them, and pinching the nipples. She moaned his name and fumbled with his waistband trying to free him.

"Off, off, off, Now Jeremy, get them off." She hopped up and pulled him to his feet.

He chuckled at her insistence and then shucked his jeans and boxers off.

Her eyes lit with delight and she took him in hand, running her palm up and down his length. Then she bent down and licked him and his knees nearly buckled from the ecstasy. She massaged his testicles with one hand and had the other hand at the base of his penis. Then, she covered the top with her hot mouth and he thought he might die from the pleasure. He grabbed her head, holding on—so he didn't collapse.

When he couldn't take the pleasure any longer he pulled on her hair. "Stop, Amber. I want to be inside you."

She gave him one last eye-crossing draw, then smiled up at him. "But, I was having fun."

"I could tell, but let's finish getting you naked and we can continue the fun."

"Okay." She released him and stood. She pulled down her zipper and dropped her slacks and panties to the floor while he stepped out of his jeans, pooled at his feet, and took off his socks. She sat on the bed to remove her socks and he cracked up. On her feet were the most hilarious socks he'd ever seen. They were yellow and covered in elephants holding trunks with little hearts between them.

"Are you laughing at my socks?" she demanded.

"How can I not? They are so funny. It never occurred to me that under your very staid uniform was weird socks—it just seems so out of character for you."

"Not at all. I have gobs of them. Just because my work clothes are rather boring does not mean that I am," she said with a huff. "I have every funny sock seller bookmarked on my computer."

"I didn't notice them when I brought you clothes. Besides, boring is not a word I would ever use in describing you. Sexy. Hot. Beautiful. Sweet. Caring. Compassionate. Did I mention sexy and hot? Even in your funny socks."

He knelt in front of her and rolled her right sock off her foot, then he kissed her ankle, her toes, her instep. She just melted back onto the bed, so he gave the left one the same attention. Kissing up the inside of her leg, he stopped and tickled the back of her knee, before going to the other leg and doing the same thing. Inching higher and higher, spreading her thighs, and coming closer and closer to the part of her that was all nerves.

He used his whiskers to scrape the inside of her thighs—not to cause pain, just a little friction to make her squirm. He spread her more, to see the pretty pink of her and then took a tiny taste. Just a little lick. She tasted amazing, so he took a bigger taste, and she pressed up against his mouth, so he obliged her and sucked her into his mouth. She moaned and it was the sexiest sound—it went straight through him, and he needed her. He needed to slide inside her hot, wet channel. So, he pulled up and she mewled in protest as he slid on the condom, but then he slid up her body and joined with her and she sighed in contentment.

She wrapped her legs around his hips and he loved her with strong, smooth strokes. He felt her body ready itself for release so he pumped into her faster and stronger.

She said, "Yes. Oh yes, Jeremy. Just like that. Yes."

When she came, she clutched at his arms and her head went back as her whole body bowed up, and he expected he might have bruises in the morning. That was his last thought, before he joined her in release—and he growled her name into her shoulder.

He rolled them to their sides, so she could breathe, and they lay there panting. When he could think again, he pulled the sheets up over her cooling body.

She muttered, "Stay with me."

"I would be happy to," he whispered back. "Just getting rid of the condom."

When he returned to the bed, he slipped in next to her. She made a happy little sound and snuggled into him, and was sound asleep. He didn't immediately fall asleep, but thought about the woman in his arms. He could get used to this, but he wondered if she felt the same way. Did he have enough to offer a woman as strong and independent as Amber was? He had to admit to himself he didn't think he did. Sure, she appreciated his willingness to help, but wouldn't any decent human being feel the same way? He didn't see it as anything special. He decided to hold on as long as she wanted him. He didn't believe that would be forever, but he would take what he could get.

CHAPTER
twenty-seven

AMBER WOKE SNUGGLED UP WITH Jeremy. She could get used to waking up with a warm, sexy man in her bed. As she lay there, she marveled at the lengths he'd gone to in order to help Owen. What a kind and sensitive man he was—and he was smart, determined. She'd known Owen for several months now, and never once thought to try to find out who he was, or if she could help him. But Jeremy had known *about* him for less than twenty-four hours and had already accomplished so much. She would be happy to stay nestled in bed with him all day, but her restaurant wouldn't run itself.

Although, maybe she should think about training someone to take over for her once in a while so she could have a few days off—or even a few mornings. Other people took time off—even other people who owned their own businesses. Definitely something to think about, but she didn't have anything in place yet, so she needed to get up. She started to untangle herself from Jeremy, but he held on tighter.

"Gotta go open the restaurant, you go back to sleep."

"Someone else can open it," he muttered, pulling her even closer.

"I was just thinking about setting that up, but it's not ready now, so I need to get up."

"No. Too lonely."

She giggled. He sounded like a little boy who was losing his best toy or blankey. She kissed him on the forehead. "I really do have to get up now. Let go and go back to sleep, I need a shower."

"Mmm hot, wet, soapy, Amber. Sounds like a fantasy. I think I better wake up and join you. I'm sure I need a shower, too."

"Well, I suppose I could spare a few minutes for shower fun, if we get a move on."

His eyes snapped open and he grinned at her. "I can do that." He practically leaped out of bed, turned around, grabbed her hand, and dragged her out of bed. She was in the shower with the water running before her brain caught up. The man could really move, when he wanted to.

They "showered" through a whole hot water tank, and only got out when the water started getting too cold. She was clean enough to go to work, but there had been a lot more fun than there had been shower.

When she finally managed to get away from Jeremy and down to her restaurant, she found it open, the coffee made, and people being served. She looked around, confused that there was nothing she needed to do to "open".

Kimberly walked up and whispered, "I saw Jeremy's Jeep out front, so I opened for you. I hope that's okay."

Amber felt her face get hot, but she nodded and smiled. "Thank you, I did have some trouble getting ready this morning."

Kimberly whispered back, "I heard the water running for a long time. You were either very dirty or had *help*."

Amber laughed. "Yeah, I suppose you could call it that."

Later that morning, the architect called and wanted to meet with her, to show her the plans he'd made up. He was planning to come to Chedwick tomorrow on the ferry, and would leave on the return trip if they were finished meeting, or spend the night if they needed more time. She agreed to meet with him as soon as he arrived, if he could meet at the restaurant. He said that would be great because he would probably be thinking about lunch by then. Amber decided to invite Jeremy, but she didn't think the entire wedding destination committee was necessary. They had all put in their two-cents-worth at the original meeting and she felt that was sufficient. It was *her* restaurant, after all.

Jeremy came in for lunch and she told him about the architect coming.

He said, "So the ferry will land about eleven thirty, and then be back to pick up returning passengers at two ten.

That's about a two-and-a-half-hour time window. You're close to the landing, so that helps. I think you need to have Marc join us as the builder, and maybe Gus, if he's helping out financially. Otherwise, both Marc and Gus will have to meet with you and/or him individually."

She sighed She hated all these group meetings, but she didn't want to have to meet with each one another time to just reiterate what was said. "You do have a point. Okay I'll ask them to join in, too. Two and a half hours should be enough, shouldn't it?"

He nodded. "Yes, as long as he didn't do anything weird, or we get some strange ideas."

"He said he was willing to stay the night if we need him to, but I don't see why we would." She really didn't want to spend her whole day in meetings.

"That's nice of him to offer, but I don't think he would need to, either."

"So, what have you been doing today?" She asked, just to keep the conversation going a little longer. She liked talking to him.

"I got some maps of the area and I was thinking maybe you would like to come over to my place and we can look at them together, to see if we can find some likely locations where Owen could be. I also called Trey and he's going to be in town permanently starting tomorrow, so I thought we could look at the maps tonight. Then, ask Trey about the places we think might be likely tomorrow or the next day."

She nodded. "That sounds good."

CHAPTER
twenty-eight

WHEN AMBER GOT TO JEREMY'S house that night, she was surprised to see it all dark. There didn't seem to be any lights on—at least not in the front of the house. She was sure he had invited her over after work to look at the maps and see if they could find some possible locations for Owen. So, why was it all dark? She hoped nothing bad had happened. She went up to the door and rang the doorbell. A few moments later, he answered the door.

"Jeremy? Are you alright?"

"Oh, Amber. Sorry I didn't know it was so late. I got a little distracted..." he rubbed his hand over the back of his neck.

"Jeremy, what's wrong?" She was starting to get worried. "Did you eat dinner?"

"I ate at your place…"

"That was lunch. Let me come in and make you something." She pushed past him and turned on a lamp, continued toward the kitchen and heard him shut the door. Good, at least he was functioning a little. She looked in the fridge and saw a few bits of food. It looked like he had enough things to make an omelet—he had three eggs, a little cheese, and some bacon. There wasn't much in the way of vegetables—a few wilted scallions and a bag of mini-carrots. She looked in the freezer and found some English muffins and a can of frozen orange juice. Good, if his blood sugar was low, and that's why he was acting so flakey, the orange juice would help.

She put the bacon in the microwave for a few minutes. It cooked faster that way and was less greasy. She made the orange juice and poured him a big glass. But she had to find him. She took the orange juice and looked in the living room. Nope, not there. So, right to the bedrooms, or left to the den. Left—his studio space was most likely in there—it would give him the most space. She walked in and found him sitting at his drafting table staring at some documents. Not turning the page and reading them, just staring at them.

She walked over. "Here, drink this." She shoved the orange juice toward him.

He looked up at her and took the orange juice and started to set it down on a coaster next to his drafting table.

"No, drink it now, Jeremy."

He shrugged. "Okay." He took a sip and started to put

it down again, but then he looked at it and brought it back to his mouth and took a big drink. After gulping down nearly the whole glass, he looked at her. "I'm starving."

"Ya think? You ate lunch at noon and it's nearly eleven. Now, put down those papers and come into the kitchen. I found almost enough food to keep a hamster alive, but it will help some."

"A hamster?" he asked, as he followed her into the kitchen.

"Hamster, mouse, bird, a few ants maybe, some small animal that might be able to survive on the tiny amount of food in your fridge. For goodness sake, Jeremy, I live above and own a restaurant and eat most of my meals there, and I have more food in my house than you do."

"Not by much. I've seen your refrigerator."

"Yes, but my freezer is stocked with things I can heat up. Yours has a few ice cubes and a couple of English muffins." The man needed a keeper; she wondered if that was the job of whatever girlfriend he was with. Since it was her he was with right now, should she just fill up his fridge? Well maybe not his fridge, but possibly his freezer. While she had no problem bossing people around about food, she wasn't sure their relationship had progressed to that stage.

"And orange juice," he said waving his glass at her. He picked up the pitcher of juice and refilled his glass.

"Yes, it did. Now it has none."

She looked at the bacon in the microwave—crisp but not over cooked. It would be perfect in his omelet. She whipped up the eggs and added some water, and poured the mixture into the skillet, added some salt and pepper. *Look at that, some garlic powder.* She added some of that, too. The English muffins went in the toaster. She chopped up the scallions and crumbled the bacon, put both of those on top of the nearly done egg mixture and added some cheese. She carefully folded half of the omelet over the other half and turned the heat off under the pan.

The English muffins popped up and she buttered them and put the jar of blueberry jelly, from the Blueberry Hills Farm in Chelan, on the table. She slid the omelet on the plate, sprinkled a bit more cheese on top, and put his plate on the table with a fork and knife.

"This looks great." He dug in. "And it tastes great. I had no idea I was so hungry."

She let him eat, because she had the thought that if she asked him what the papers were all about he would stop eating. So, she just waited while he shoveled the food into his mouth like a lumberjack.

When he finished every bit and pushed his plate away, he grinned at her. "That was delicious. Thanks for cooking for me."

"You're welcome, Maybe you could order a few foodstuffs to put in that refrigerator or at least the freezer."

"I could probably order a few things from Safeway, if you're going to be around to cook once in a while."

She ignored his innuendo. "So, what were those papers you were staring at?"

A scowl covered his face. "Nothing important."

Nothing important? Oh, for goodness sake. *Nothing important* didn't shut a person down for hours. She huffed. "Jeremy, you'd been sitting in the dark staring at them for hours. Tell me."

"Oh, just a new contract to write graphic novels for the *Adventures with Tsilly* game."

"I thought you liked that idea." Hadn't they talked about this already? He didn't freak out last time.

"It's interesting, but this contract has tight deadlines and large deliverables. I don't think I'm the right person for it."

"Oh, don't be silly. You would be great at it."

"No, I wouldn't." He stood up and stalked out of the room.

Amber felt like he'd slapped her. What the hell? She followed him into his study where he was standing at the window staring off into the darkness. She went up and put her arms around his waist and her head on his back.

"Jeremy, talk to me. What's wrong?"

"I can't do it. I'm an imposter. All those children's books aren't mine."

"What do you mean? Of course they are."

He turned from the window and grabbed her arms, pushing her back from him. He looked her in the eye and said, "No, they aren't mine. Yes, I produce them, but none of the stories are mine. None of the pictures. I didn't invent the characters and I don't make up the stories. A focus group does. They take the new version of the game and give me a story template. They select the theme of the book and how the story will go, and they give me a list of the books to produce.

"I take the characters Sandy and Steve created and draw them, doing whatever the script says they should do. Now, a new focus group comes along and they want me to create graphic novels. Graphic novels are a hundred times more complex, and I have no idea where to start. I can't do it." He gave her a small shake. "Don't you see? Everyone thinks I'm this hotshot author and in reality, I'm an automaton that does what someone else tells me to do."

Oh, good lord. He's a basket case. She saw one of his stories and picked it up and opened it to a page. "So, you're telling me that someone, some focus group, tells you to draw Kalar standing on this rock, in this outfit, with her sword drawn?" She pointed to the corner of the page. "They tell you to draw this little bunny in this corner munching on grass and that blue and gray bird flying overhead?"

He sighed and shook his head. "No, not in that detail. They tell me what the story is about. I draw the individual pages."

"Okay, so they tell you what words to put on this page? Like this one?"

"No, I determine what's on each page—both the pictures and the words."

"Well, that sounds like you do some of the creating."

Jeremy rolled his eyes. "Yes I suppose I do some of it, but it's still not my characters or my plot."

"Have you ever written a book with your own characters and plot? Maybe it's not all it's cracked up to be."

"I have, yes." He looked toward a filing cabinet in the corner. "But it's not published. I did it just for myself."

"Then, I seem to be missing something here. You are given the plot and characters for the Tsilly kids' books, but you determine what the dialogue is and what the pictures look like. You are capable of writing your own books and have done so. Now, the game company wants you to write longer, more involved books, and you're all freaked out about it. What am I missing?"

"I just don't know if I can do it. If I sign my name to this contract, I'll be agreeing to do something that I don't even know if I am capable of doing."

Still not seeing what the big deal was, she asked, "Okaaay, and if you fail and can't complete the contract or even the first graphic novel, what happens?"

"I'll be a failure."

"And the game company will what? Come burn down your house and shoot you at dawn?"

"Don't be ridiculous," he said crossing his arms and scowling at her.

"Okay, fine. Then what would happen? Enlighten me."

"Well, if they give me an advance and I don't deliver they could ask for the advance back."

"And you can't afford to give it back?" She was pretty sure he was rolling in cash so that didn't make sense. What was really going on here?

Jeremy put his hands on his hips. "Of course, I can. Besides they probably wouldn't. They would probably just put it toward the next group of kids' books."

"Then nothing would really happen. You just go back to your cushy job as a famous author, granted one that doesn't have a lot of say in things, but it's still a pretty good job."

"Except, I would be a failure."

She shrugged. "Then don't sign it. I don't give a hot damn if you do or not. If you want to try it then do, and if you don't then don't. Seems pretty simple to me."

Jeremy gaped at her. Then a slow smile slid across his face. "You're right, I can do it or not, it's my choice. And even if I try it and fail, who cares. I'll just go back to doing the kids books."

"Exactly." Glad he was not so conflicted and drawn to that smile, she nodded.

"You're amazing. You take all these boiling feelings and distill them down to the essence. I love that about you."

She snapped her gaze up to his. "What?"

"I love that about you. But, no. It's bigger than that. I just plain love you. And I think that scares the crap out of me."

"I know it scares the crap out of me. You can't just go around saying I love you all willy-nilly like." She poked him in the chest.

"It's not willy-nilly. It's been building for days now, to where I can't deny it any longer."

"But..." She didn't know what to say, she was so confused on how she felt about him and how she felt about his feelings.

"No buts, I know how I feel and you aren't in charge of

that. You're only in charge of your own feelings and there is no need, whatsoever, to decide what those are at this time. In fact, I don't want you to. Let's just stick with my feelings and leave it, for now. Sooo, do you want to look at the maps or go to bed and make love?"

"After that declaration, I think we have to go to bed. Poring over maps just doesn't seem like the thing to do."

"Sounds like a fine idea to me—going to bed that is." He grinned at her.

She started babbling, still confused about his declaration. "Excellent, why don't you put the maps in your Jeep and we can look at them tomorrow after the meeting with the architect. I'm getting Tammy O'Connor to come in tomorrow to help, so I can take some time off. Since we're meeting onsite, they can always come get me if they need to, but Tammy can be there to pick up the slack now that she's finally feeling better. That pneumonia knocked her flat."

"Yeah, it was a hard way for Chris to find out she was so sick, but it's a good thing he did. If Irene hadn't pulled all those shenanigans on Chris and Barbara, Tammy might have died. You just never know when something awful is really a blessing in disguise. But hasn't she been working at the art gallery with Kristen?"

"Yeah, she worked a lot more in the summer, but now it's just a few days a week. She's free tomorrow. So, now. Where were we on all that going to bed stuff?" she said as she pressed against him and pulled his mouth down to hers. "Take me to bed, Jeremy."

CHAPTER
twenty-nine

JEREMY WOKE TO AN EMPTY BED. He'd known she would have to leave early to open the restaurant, but it was still disappointing. How she managed on so little sleep was a mystery to him—he needed a good eight hours to make him feel normal. Sometimes, those eight were at random times of the day since he worked when he was feeling motivated and then slept when he got too tired to think. But he didn't think she'd gotten even four hours last night. They'd made love several times in the wee hours of the morning. Now that he thought about it, she'd probably left after they'd woken up about four and had slowly driven each other wild. That had been a very pleasant interlude— very pleasant, indeed.

He got up and headed for the shower. As he stood

under the hot water he thought about the graphic novel contract. His mind drifted and he started to see a story come together in his brain. He grabbed the waterproof notepad he kept in the shower and the pencil and started drawing the idea in his head.

When he ran out of paper he swore and noticed the water was ice cold and he was actually shivering. His shower wall was filled with little notes that stuck to the wet tiles. He was about a third of the way through what looked like it might be a decent graphic novel. He rinsed in the frigid water and turned it off, grabbed a towel and quickly rubbed it over his body and hair. After throwing on some jeans, he carefully took the notes off the wall, in order, and took them to his office. He grabbed one of the cardboard display boards that doubled as a plotting board and laid the notes out on it. They didn't stick to cardboard so he had to use thumb tacks to attach them.

The large sticky notes were about the same size, so he grabbed a couple of pads of them and started where he'd left off. Two hours later, he had the whole story plotted and sketched out. He stood up and felt his back groan in protest. The phone was ringing and beeping and just going crazy and he was starving and cold. He picked up the phone and answered it.

"Jeremy, where are you?" Amber screeched. "It's noon. The architect is here and so are Gus and Marc. Are you coming?"

He looked down at his bare chest and feet. "Yes, I'll be there in five minutes. Sorry, I got caught up."

"Okay, I'll stall them with food and pretend like it was planned this way, but hurry the hell up, will you."

"Yes, ma'am. Can you save me some of the food? I haven't eaten since you fed me last night."

"Oh, for the love of Pete. Yes, I'll order you something. You haven't been brooding again have you?"

"No, quite the opposite. See you in a few." He hung up and started moving fast. In five minutes, he had to get dressed, grab his portfolio, the maps, his backpack, and drive over to Amber's.

He made it in twelve minutes. He charged in the door with his portfolio in one hand and his backpack in the other. The smell of roast beef made his stomach cramp and rumble in protest to his harsh treatment. Kimberly pointed to the fine dining side of the restaurant and rolled her eyes at him. He walked over there and saw Amber had set up a nice area for the meeting. Everyone was busy eating hot roast beef sandwiches with mashed potatoes and gravy.

"Sorry I'm late I have a very demanding muse and she wasn't about to let me get away until I finished plotting."

Wes laughed. "Oh, the suffering we artists must endure. Even in architecture, which should be rather straight forward, I find the creative personality driving me to get it just right before I am free to live."

"Thanks for understanding. It all started in the shower."

"Of course, it did. Where probably ninety five percent of all inspiration happens. Then, or just as you start to drift off to sleep." Wes chuckled. "So, do you have a water proof notepad or did you have to get out of the shower?"

"I had—emphasis on had—a water proof notepad. Now it's empty and the pencil is a stub."

Amber interrupted the exchange. "Sit down and eat, Jeremy. I can hear your stomach rumbling from here."

He wasn't about to argue, so he dropped his bags, sat down, and started stuffing his face.

When they all had finished eating, the architect revealed his plans, and everyone loved them. Marc looked over the construction blueprints carefully. Wes had printed out a copy of the CAD drawings—some people still liked to hold the paper in their hands. Amber looked at the BIM drawings. She could look at every angle and into every nook—it was amazing to her to see what the Building Information Management software could do. It was nearly like walking through the building. It was going to be amazing. Jeremy talked shop with Wes and Gus looked over the approximate cost.

After a half hour, Gus cleared his throat. "Can y'all sit back down for a minute? Amber can you get Tammy to bring us in a bite of dessert?"

"It should be here any minute, Gus."

Gus nodded and everyone took their seats. "So, Marc, when would you be able to get started on this? Do you have a demolition team to start taking the ruined pieces out?"

"I do have a team that can start on that right away. My renovations team is about finished with the changes Mayor Carol wanted on her house for the B&B. There's likely to be a few things that need to be done there. But, we should have the bulk finished by the time all the burned out materials are removed from Amber's. Have we been cleared to begin, Amber?"

"Yes, I believe so. I've received the insurance money. It won't pay for this elaborate plan, but it will help with some of the needs. I don't know if there are any issues with the fire investigator," she said, looking toward Jeremy.

"Nope, no issues. You're free to start I confirmed that after you told me about the meeting today."

Gus said, "Well, I plan to foot the bill for whatever is needed that the insurance company check can't cover, so let's git 'er done."

⚭

WHEN EVERYONE HAD eaten their pie and gone on their way, Amber said to Jeremy, "Upstairs. Bring your maps and other crap."

She walked into the reception area and told Kimberly, "I'm going upstairs, I'm done. I'll try to be back down for the dinner rush."

"If you want that's fine, but I'm not busy today at all so I can stay. And Candy and Janine will be showing up any minute, so I don't know that we really need you so much. You could take the night off."

"I'm not sure I would know how to act with a night off."

Kimberly raised her eyebrows. "I see Jeremy heading toward your apartment, I'm sure you could find *something* to keep you occupied."

Amber smirked. "I have no idea what you're talking about, but I think I will take you up on that offer and take the evening off. Call me if something happens and I need to come down."

"Will do, but don't expect it."

When she got upstairs with Jeremy, she told him she was going to put on some sweats since Kimberly was certain they wouldn't need her downstairs tonight. Once she was comfortable, she came out to find he'd set out the maps of the area on her table. There was a large one that showed the whole area and several others that showed more detail of smaller sections.

"Can we look at those in a little while? I just want to sit on the couch for a few minutes and relax. I was kind of tense going into this meeting today. When you didn't show up on time and didn't answer your phone right away, I got a little freaked out. So, I just need to decompress for a few minutes." She walked in and flopped on the couch.

"I'm sorry I caused you more stress. I just got caught up." He sat next to her and took her hand in his.

"So, what happened?"

"You know the graphic novel I was crazed about? Well, in the middle of my shower the whole thing just downloaded into my brain. I grabbed the water-proof notepad all authors should have in their shower and started drawing up sketches of what I was thinking. When I ran out of paper, I realized the water had long gone cold. So, I put on some jeans, took my water notes, and started using sticky notes to finish the story. When I finally finished the story, I heard my phone ringing and text messages coming in and answered. I just didn't hear it before then. Maybe my subconscious did, but definitely not the part of my brain that would stop to answer it."

She frowned. "What if the house had caught on fire or there was an emergency?"

"I've trained my brain to respond to emergencies and the fire scanner. But everything else? Not so much."

"So, if I'd walked in naked you wouldn't have noticed?"

"I don't think I would go that far. Do you want to come over and experiment? I could pretend to be the hard-working author and you could try to seduce me away from my work." He looked at her with a pretend air of innocence.

She laughed. "Well, not today."

"Drats."

"Anyway, back to the graphic novel. I thought you didn't want any part of it?"

"No, it wasn't that. I just didn't know if I would be able to come up with a good story. But once I decided it wouldn't be a life or death scenario if I didn't, I guess it freed my mind." He shrugged.

"So, why haven't you tried to publish your other children's books?" She shifted on the couch so she was facing him.

"I don't think anyone would buy them."

"But, you haven't tried."

"No, and I don't plan to. I did them just for me." He crossed his arms over his chest. He was very protective about his stories—they meant too much to him.

"Will you show them to me? Next time we're at your house?"

"No, they're not good enough."

She wheedled, "Come on, it's just me. It's not like I'm some big shot New York publisher. I'm just a waitress-turned-restaurant owner."

"Well, I'll think about it."

"Maybe I could think up a reward system." She tapped her finger to her lip. "I know, we'll play strip story reading. I'll take off one article of clothing for each story you let me read. How many are there?"

A hot look came into his eyes at that suggestion, which made her body flood with lust. He cleared his throat. "I have several things written. Let's start with the children's books. There are seven of them. But, it somehow seems wrong to have you stripping while reading children's story books."

"Well, I won't be reading them to children."

He laughed. "Thank God for that. They might get an education that is not the intent of the books. And now I'm all hot and bothered from imagining it." He took her arm and started pulling her toward his lap.

She laughed and pulled away. "Oh, well, we need to look at those maps now. Would a cold beer cool you down? Or I have some iced tea made."

"Actually, the iced tea sounds good."

"Let's head for the kitchen and we'll see if we can find some likely locations where Owen might be hiding."

They looked over the maps and found some ideas based on things Hank had told them about Owen's past.

CHAPTER
thirty

THE NEXT MORNING JEREMY called Trey Peterson, the hotshot that was staying in town, to see if he had time to talk to him and Hank. He said he had time that morning and then that afternoon he was meeting with clients that needed websites built.

Jeremy called Hank's cell number and he answered on the first ring. "Hey, Hank. This is Jeremy."

"Jeremy. What can I do for you?"

"I talked to Trey, the hotshot from the forest fires. And I was wondering if you have time to meet with him and me, to look over some maps and see if we can find some likely locations where Owen might be."

Hank cleared his throat. "I'll make time for that, Jeremy. That's too important to ignore. Winters coming soon and I'd like to get him taken care of before that. But, would it be possible to look them over here at the ranch?"

He agreed with Hank—the sooner they found Owen the better they would all feel. "Sure, that would be fine. Both Trey and I have commitments this afternoon."

"This morning works. Come on over anytime. I won't be far from the barn—it's right in the middle of fall-calving, so I'm sticking close for that and making winter plans."

"See you in a bit."

Jeremy picked up Trey at Mary Ann's house. "Hey, Trey. Thanks for taking some time for this."

"No problem. This is my new home town, so I need to be a part of it—and if that means looking for a vet down on his luck, I'm there."

"New home town? So, you and Mary Ann are..."

Trey said easily, "I plan to marry that woman, as soon as I can convince her of that idea. So, yes. This is my permanent home town. I'll still probably have to go other places during fire season, but the rest of the year, I'm here."

Marriage was a big commitment, but Trey seemed laid back about the idea. Jeremy wondered how he felt about marriage. Did he feel like this thing with Amber was leading that way? Quite possibly. "Good thing you have such a flexible career during the off season."

"Yeah, and this town has a shit ton of work for me. I think every single business owner has cornered me asking for web page development. Plus, the town and several special interest groups, like the artisans, want a group page—and now the destination wedding team. But you probably know that since you're one of the artisans and you're dating one of the wedding team."

"Yeah, I've heard plenty. But dragging Amber into the world of the web is not going to be an easy task. She and her restaurant are pretty old school."

Trey laughed. "She won't be my first challenge. I'll get her going. I can draw her in slowly."

"Not sure she's the slowly type, but we'll just have to wait and see how it goes."

When they drove into the ranch, Hank looked up, waved, and walked over to them. "Hi guys. I think it's safe to use the dining room. Beth's at school."

Jeremy laughed and Trey looked confused. Jeremy said, "The last time I was here his eight-year-old daughter, Beth, tried to convince me she needed to be the heroine in her very own Tsilly book. She was quite adamant about it, and we finally had to go lock ourselves into the barn to get away from her."

"She must be quite the pistol." Trey grinned.

Hank nodded. "Yes, she is."

Jeremy looked at Hank. "I'm going to be writing a graphic novel, and my heroine in the story is named Beth and looks like a slightly grown up version of your daughter. She may be a little too young for it now, but my guess is it won't be out for at least a year, probably two. The publishing industry is notoriously slow."

Hank shook his head. "Probably not too young, she's in third grade and is a good reader."

"Oh, well. In that case, maybe she can be a beta reader."

"She would love that," Hank said.

They went in the back door and hung their coats in the mud room. The ground was dry, so they didn't need to worry about their shoes. The dining room Hank led them to had good lighting from the large windows that looked into the back yard.

Jeremy set his backpack of supplies down, got the maps out of the portfolio and laid them on the table. "I got an overall map of the whole area and some more detailed smaller maps."

"Do you mind if we draw on these?" Trey asked.

Jeremy nodded. "I got some blueprint covers that will protect the maps and we can draw on them with felt tip pens or grease pencils. I have felt tip pens."

"Perfect. I was thinking we could start by outlining where the fire was on the big map and I can show you places we found odd things."

"Sounds like a plan," Hank chimed in.

While Trey started on the big map, Jeremy and Hank took the more detailed ones and added in the things they knew about. They also filled Trey in on Owen and what they knew about him.

Trey looked up from the map. "So, Owen is the one that caused the fire in Amber's banquet room? Is she going to press charges? Are you calling it arson?"

"No, we aren't calling it arson. We're fairly certain it was an accident, those chip bags go up easily and the banquet room was pretty close quarters, so it wouldn't take long to spread. Amber is worried about Owen and is not going to press charges. It would be nice to hear Owen's side of the story, so we can put it all to rest."

"Well, let's see if we can find him before winter really arrives," Hank said.

They went over the maps, the information that Trey had, and the guesses Amber and Jeremy had thought of. They picked several likely spots he could be and decided they could hit two a day using the mornings. That would leave them all the afternoons to work. They could go to some of them by Jeep, some by four wheelers, and some would require horses. They thought they had a good plan of attack.

Jeremy dropped Trey off and decided he would have lunch at Amber's before he went home to look at the plotting for the graphic novel and if he was happy with it, to call his agent.

"Hi Jeremy," Amber said when she had time to stop by his table. "You are just the person I wanted to see. I've been thinking about it all morning. So, can I come over this afternoon during my lull and read your non-Tsilly children's books?"

Jeremy felt his gut clench at that idea. He didn't know if he was ready to share them, or if he ever would be. "I'm going to be working on the graphic novel to see if it's something I'm willing to commit to, so…"

"Oh, good. Then I can read them while you do that."

Damn, not the reaction I'm going for. "Well, I guess it would be okay."

She clapped her hands. "Oh, goody. So, did you meet with Hank and Trey this morning?"

He took another bite of his French dip and nodded. "Yes, we have a number of spots to look at. We're going to try spending mornings searching for him and then we can all work in the afternoons. Different areas will require different access so we're grouping them that way, and also by proximity."

"Nice. You sound very well organized. I wish I could go with you, but mornings and evenings are my busiest times." She wrung her hands.

"Don't worry, I'll keep you in the loop." He smiled at her concern for her friend. She was such a sweetheart—no wonder he'd fallen in love with her.

"Every day?"

He drained his iced tea. "Every day. Lunch was delicious, but I've got work to do."

"Thanks, and I better get busy, too. I'll see you this afternoon." She smiled like he had promised her a trip to Paris.

Damn, I hope she forgets. He shrugged trying to pull off nonchalance. "If you have time."

"I will *make* time," she said with a determined smile on her face.

And that was exactly what he was afraid of.

CHAPTER
thirty-one

AMBER HUSTLED OUT OF THE RESTAURANT and got in her car. She knew Jeremy wasn't excited about her reading his original stories, but she was excited enough for both of them. She just knew they would be amazing. If they were as good as she imagined, she was determined to get him to submit them for publication. Then he wouldn't feel like an imposter any longer.

She drove into his driveway, and stopped to admire his home. It was a little separated from other houses in the area, up on a slight hill, which gave him a partial view of Lake Chelan from the front of his house, and a magnificent view of the Cascade mountains in the back. It wasn't a huge house, but plenty big for one guy. She thought it was custom made, especially since his studio was huge—she'd noticed that much the other day when she'd come over. His yard could use some work. It was late enough in the season that it didn't matter that much, but there were some flowers that were being choked out by weeds.

She went up and rang the doorbell. It took him a few minutes, but he answered.

"Hi, Amber."

"How's it going?"

He stepped back and she walked into the foyer. "Good, actually. I still like the story I came up with in the shower yesterday. I'm doing up a prototype to send my agent and the game company." He took her jacket and hung it on the coat rack. "It won't be the final art, but enough to give everyone an idea of where I'm going, and give the focus group something to tear apart."

She flinched. "Is it really that bad?"

"No, not really. Well, sometimes, at least, that's the way it feels."

"Bummer. No wonder you're reluctant to show your other work to people." She kicked off her shoes. "But, I promise I won't tear it apart."

He laughed, but it sounded a little bitter. "Come on in, then. I put the little kids' series next to the seating area, so you can be comfortable."

She followed him into his studio and went over to the seating area he indicated. He had put out a glass of iced tea, his manuscripts, a red felt tip pen and some document flags. She turned toward him, he had gone back to his drafting table. "What's with the felt pen and sticky flags?"

"So you can mark up anything you don't like."

"Jeremy, I didn't come to critique your stories—just to read them."

He shrugged. "I'm sure you'll find something that's awkward."

"I'm not sure of that at all." She shook her head. He really was insecure about his work.

"But if you do, you can mark it."

Amber frowned at his attitude, but sat down to start reading. She curled her legs up under her and picked up the first book. "Jeremy, why does this have a different author name on it? Who is Allen Andrews?"

"I was originally going to send them in to my agent and publisher, but I didn't want them to be part of the Tsilly phenomenon so I created a pen name. I used my middle name Allen and mother's maiden name Andrews."

She nodded and looked back down at the book in her hands. It was a story about a little boy and his adventures in his yard. Where a puddle of water became a large lake and the flower bed turned into a huge forest. He was hunting for wild animals to make friends with. It was such a cute story and she laughed at his antics. The artwork was so fun, showing what it really looked like on the left of each page, and what the little boy imagined on the right.

The second book was just as entertaining, where the carpet inside the house was lava, and the little boy had to traverse across the room to save his companion, a giant lion—stuffed, of course. He had to find ways to cross the lava without being burned. She remembered Chris and herself playing that same game when they were young, and wondered if all children did that. It would make the book great fun to read for all ages because of the nostalgia from doing the same.

She got so caught up in reading the books, she forgot about the felt tip pens and the flags—and even the iced tea.

JEREMY COULDN'T GET back into the graphic novel he was working on. He just watched Amber as she read his stories. He had tried to ignore her, but every chuckle and every sigh made him look up. She seemed to be enjoying his books and she hadn't once picked up the red felt pen or the doc flags.

She must have felt him watching her, because she looked up at him with a smile on her face. "Jeremy, these are wonderful. You need to share them with the world."

"I'm glad you like them, Amber. But they're not good enough for the world." He looked back down at his drafting table to cut her off. He just couldn't take the rejection of sending them out and having an editor or his agent chew them up and spit them out. They were too close to his heart to have someone try to change them. They reminded him of his childhood and since he didn't have any family left to reminisce with anymore, he needed them to stay the way they were.

He needed to forget about Amber reading them and work on this graphic novel. He wanted to have the first cut done and in his agent's hands by the end of the month. He picked up his pen and started inking the panels he'd already penciled in. That way, he didn't have to concentrate so much—it was a more mechanical process. With Amber there distracting him, it would be better than trying to continue the story.

He probably should be doing all this work on his computer, but sometimes he just had to use pencil and paper. Yeah, he'd have to scan it in later, but he needed the tactile feel of it. He felt more creative. He'd read articles that agreed with his gut—that said people were more creative on paper.

He'd finally gotten back in the groove and was getting a lot done when Amber sighed.

She put the last book down and turned to him, "Jeremy you need to publish those. They are wonderful."

"Amber—"

"No. Now you listen to me. The world needs these books. Even as an adult I was drawn back to my childhood by reading them. Every kid does these same things and the way you've described and drawn them is magical. You have to publish them."

"I love them, too, Amber. And that's why I won't send them to an agent or editor—because they always want things changed based on the market and previous works. And frankly, I don't want to change them."

She could understand that. She wouldn't want them changed. "Can't you self-publish then?"

"Not really. My contract with my agent is pretty tight."

"Even under a different pen name?" she questioned. She wasn't going to let him brush this off.

"I don't know. I just don't think I want to put myself out there for criticism on these. And I don't have the time to jump through all the hoops right now, with the graphic novel and searching for Owen and…"

"But—"

"No buts, Amber. Just drop it."

Dammit, she had no intention of dropping it, but she would back off today. "Fine. Well, I better get back to work."

"I am glad you liked them, though."

"It's more than that, Jeremy. I loved them and I know other people—"

"Yeah, I've heard you loud and clear." He got up and took her hand. "I'll walk you to the door."

When they got to the door, he pulled her in and gave her a warm kiss. "I might stay working on the graphic novel the rest of today, so I may not see you tonight. But after we look for Owen tomorrow, I'll stop into the diner."

"I'll see you tomorrow, then."

As she drove away, Amber fumed. She knew she'd pushed him too hard, but those books needed to be published. They were too good to gather dust in the bottom of some filing cabinet. *Stupid man.* No, he wasn't stupid. But he did have a confidence issue—that much was certain.

All his books had charmed her, but two of them stood out—the one with the carpet being lava and the second one was about the little boy and his side-kick, which was, surprisingly, a beaver. He and the beaver were camping. The tent was blankets and towels draped over dining room furniture, exactly like she and Chris had done.

The little boy and his beaver were on a scouting party mapping the wilderness. They came upon strange new beasts and amazing lands and even a few people. When they needed to cross a river the beaver would quickly chew down some trees and the little boy would lash them together with some trusty rope he carried. It gave them a bridge across the water.

How could anyone not love those stories? He needed to publish them, but she had no idea how to convince him to try. Maybe something would come to her. She had every intention of making sure those books got into the hands of people.

CHAPTER
thirty-two

For the next few days Amber saw Jeremy at lunch. They weren't having much luck finding Owen. They'd gone to all the places that the Jeep or four wheelers could get to, with no luck. Jeremy was spending all his afternoons working on the graphic novel and Amber knew it was irrational, but she felt lonely only seeing him at lunch. She missed his company. Work had started on the banquet room, so she was busy, but it just didn't feel right without him being around. She'd gotten used to him, and she wondered if he felt the same. Deciding to find out, she told her staff she would be in for the lunch rush tomorrow, but not for breakfast.

Amber put her overnight bag in her car and drove to Jeremy's house. She'd stopped by Samantha's bakery and got some of the cinnamon rolls he liked for breakfast with plenty of butter and icing, and instructions on how to warm them up. Then cover them in the icing and butter, so that they would be fresh—just like he got them in the morning.

When he answered the door, he looked surprised to see her—pleased but surprised. "Um, did I forget you were coming over?"

"Nope, I just decided I missed you and you had no choice in the matter."

A slow smile spread across his face and her knees got weak. "You missed me?"

"Yes, I brought an overnight bag and breakfast from Samantha's for in the morning."

"You don't have to work?"

"I told them I'd be in for lunch." She ran one finger down his chest, which was bare. Apparently, he liked working shirtless.

"Oh. So, no need to hurry out of bed. That sounds promising... Damn, but we're taking the horses out tomorrow to look for Owen."

"What time?"

"We're meeting at nine." He frowned.

"Plenty of time. I'm an early riser you know."

He grinned. "I do. Come on into my studio, I just need to finish one small thing."

She followed him into his studio and over to a big machine he had some of his drawings on. "What are you doing?"

"Scanning in the pages I have done on the graphic novel. Some people draw them right on the computer, but I like paper better. So, once they're ready, I have to scan them onto the computer to mail to my agent and the game company. They don't want paper these days."

"That's kinda cool. Did you do that with my menu?"

"Yes, let me show you." He opened up his file explorer and showed her where her menu was stored. It was under the folder name "Amber - children menu", she saw other folders with the names of other books he'd written including the ones she'd read the other night.

"Oh, so all your books are on here? And then you what? Email them to your agent and the game company?"

He seemed pleased she was interested in his process, so he showed her the email, too. "Yes, and the publisher. So, I send it to my agent and the game company first, and then they send me back changes, and then when everyone's happy I send it to the publisher. The publisher could still have changes, but not too often because the other two know what they want and what the publisher is willing to produce."

"Wow, that's a lot more complicated than I thought it would be. So, if the game company wasn't involved would you just do the agent and publisher? Like for someone who wasn't writing books for a game." Many more steps than she had imagined and a lot of fingers in the pie. No wonder he felt beat up, if everyone got to make changes to his work.

He nodded. "Yes, some people only work with agents

and let them farm out the book to see which publisher would take it, but I'm established with one publisher, so my agent just helps with the changes and brokers the money side of things."

"This is fascinating. I read books when I have time, and I had no idea what all goes into it."

"Yeah, for some people they have to have an illustrator and cover designer, but I do my own. For adult books, there's also a formatter and an editor and a proofreader. If there are people on the covers, like for romances, there are cover models and a photographer, too. There's a lot of people involved in creating a book."

She shook her head. "I never knew."

"Most people don't and that's fine, but for those of us in the business there's a lot more than just writing a story."

Very interesting, but she hadn't come here to talk all night about the publishing world. "Cool, so what do you need to finish before I can drag you off and have my wicked way with you?"

"I just need to scan in these last two pages and then the chapter is complete."

"Okay, you do that while I go put our breakfast in the kitchen. And then I'll get more comfortable, you come and join me when you're finished."

She barely got to his room before he joined her. "I thought it would take you a little longer to get finished."

"I was highly motivated."

"Well, I suppose I do owe you a strip tease for letting

me read your stories. I think that's what we talked about, wasn't it?"

He swallowed loudly. "You don't need to do that. It was us just kidding around."

"Oh, but I want to. So, you just sit down and get ready to enjoy the show."

He grinned and sat on the bed.

For all her big talk, she was a little nervous about this. She'd never stripped for a man before, but she wanted to rock his world and she was determined to do so. "Close your eyes."

He did as he was told and Amber slipped the sky-high heels out of her bag and traded them for the flats she had worn to drive over—there was no way she could drive in those shoes.

"You can open your eyes now."

He took in her CFM footwear and his eyes heated. "Love the shoes." His voice was a little rough sounding, which made her bold.

Her sweater and slacks were very innocent looking but what she had on underneath was pure sin and she was excited to watch Jeremy's reaction as it was revealed. The sweater was V-necked with little buttons down the front. She started slipping each one slowly out of its buttonhole. As each one unfastened it allowed the sweater to gap a little more than the last. When she undid the last button she ran her hands through her hair fluffing it but also causing the sweater to open even farther.

She pulled the shoulder down on one side so the fire

engine red of her bra strap was visible. He watched her like a hawk. His jaw tightened with each tiny bit of skin that was revealed and she reveled in her femininity.

She let the other shoulder slip and the sweater to fall to the floor. He groaned when her bright red lace demi bra was fully revealed.

Next, she started on the slacks, unbuttoning the waistband and sliding the zipper down slowly. With each click of the zipper, she saw him get a little more tense. When she stopped and then shimmied her hips to let the slacks drop to the floor she thought he might swallow his tongue when her barely there panties and thigh high lace stockings came into view.

He groaned, "You're trying to kill me, aren't you?"

"No. Not at all. Just getting your attention." She let a sultry laugh come out of her throat as she stepped out of the slacks and one step closer to him. "That's only two of the seven articles of clothing, you have five more to go."

"Well, that outfit you have on now is plenty hot enough to get my blood boiling. The red sex-wear with the thigh stockings and come fuck me shoes. Lord, woman. You are hot."

She smiled at his appreciation and unclasped her bra and let it slide down to the floor.

He swallowed audibly as she ran her hands over her bare breasts. "Can I help?"

"No sir, you just sit there and watch." She moved closer and lifted one foot to the bed between his legs. "Actually, you can help, please take my shoe off."

He carefully removed her shoe and she let her foot scoot forward to caress him through his jeans. He was rock hard. She wiggled her foot just a bit more and then put in on the floor and lifted the second one to do the same.

She lifted her legs one at a time placing each foot on his thigh, to roll her stocking down each leg, he was practically steaming he was so hot and she was drenched. When both stockings had been rolled slowly down her legs, she stepped back wearing only her red panties and pretended to count on her fingers. "Well that's all seven articles of clothing. Guess we're done." Then, she turned around to walk away.

He growled and grabbed her arm, whirling her back around. "Now it's my turn, woman."

Then, he crashed his mouth down on hers and filled his hands with her breasts. He backed her up until her she was against the wall and pushed his pelvis into hers grinding himself against her. It was fabulous—she'd accomplished what she'd set out to do, and that was to drive him mad with desire.

When he pulled back, he said gruffly, "That was by far the hottest thing I have ever seen Amber."

She looked at him with a wicked smile. "Good. Now, let's continue this strip show—with you losing some clothes."

He stepped back whipped his jeans and shorts off so fast it was a blur. "Gladly."

Then, he knelt before her and kissed her through her wet panties and dragged them down her legs, dropped them to the floor, and flipped her over his shoulder to carry her to the bed where he dropped her. She bounced as he grabbed a condom out of the night stand, had it on, and was down on top of her so fast it took her breath away. He entered her in one long plunge and she wrapped her legs around his hips.

He loved her with long smooth strokes until she came apart in ecstasy and then he joined her on that path to the heights of pleasure.

As they lay together, their bodies cooling, she reveled in the way he had responded to her. She had never done anything like that before, but he'd made it perfectly clear that her performance was everything she had hoped it would be.

He pulled her close and wrapped his arms and legs around her. His voice was gruff when he said, "That was by far the most erotic thing I have ever seen. I believe that will be one of the most memorable and amazing activities of my life. Thank you for wanting to give me that."

She sighed and wrapped her arms and legs around him, too. "You responded exactly as I had hoped you would."

He chuckled. "How could I not? You are amazing. Let's rest a while before round two."

"Round two?"

"Oh, yes. With that hot strip show going round and round in my head, there's liable to be a round three, four and five."

She shivered at the thought. "Then, we better rest in between."

They spent the night alternating between sleep and making love. They ended up eating the cinnamon rolls about four o'clock in the morning because they were starving from all the activity. Then, they made love again and went back to sleep wrapped around each other.

CHAPTER
thirty-three

JEREMY KISSED AMBER. "I'VE GOT TO go meet the guys now. You kick back and enjoy the morning off—you don't have to rush out. My house is your house. In fact, let me give you a key."

"You don't need to do that."

"No, it's a good idea. I sometimes get caught up and don't hear knocking or even the doorbell. So, if you have a key you can just come in." He opened a kitchen drawer and rummaged around for a few seconds. "Ah, here it is. Now you can have a relaxing morning and lock up when you're ready to leave."

"Thanks, I don't get a chance to take it slow most mornings, so I'll do as suggested." She grinned.

"Wish I could stay with you…"

"I know, but finding Owen is more important. We'll have other late mornings once he's found." She would love to have him stay longer, too, but she was worried about Owen.

"I'm going to hold you to that." The tone of his voice and the look in his eye made her shiver.

"You do that. Now get going. Good luck. I hope today's the day you find him." He kissed her once more and then was out the door.

She filled up her coffee cup and wandered toward his studio. She was a little achy from all the amorous activity in the night, but she reveled even in that. It was a night to remember.

She went over to look at his graphic novel pages he had finished scanning last night. Even in his haste, he was meticulously organized. The chapter he'd been working on was clipped together and put in a pile with the other chapters that were finished. She read the page on top and thought it looked like a great story.

When she set her coffee cup on his desk she bumped the mouse. His computer woke up and his email came up. There was a second account below his main one that had the author name for the set of books he'd allowed her to read. Did she dare open it? No, that would be an invasion of his privacy. She turned her back on the computer and looked at the second page of the graphic novel. Her eyes scanned the panels, but she didn't remember a single word—her brain was focused on that other email account.

She could just look at what was inside it. That

wouldn't hurt anything. She looked around to make sure no one was watching, not sure who she was looking for. She laughed at herself and clicked on the second account. There was nothing in it. Disappointment filled her heart. She'd wanted to find evidence that he had sent those files. The drafts folder had a number by it. She clicked on it and found the emails ready with attachments for the books she had read and another second set of draft emails with a second series.

She clicked on one of those drafts and read the cover letter email. That series was for older kids and he'd said they were chapter books for school aged children. There was a third set of emails and when she clicked on that one, the email said they were young adult books. That surprised her—young adults don't read picture books. *Now that I think about it, I don't think chapter books have many pictures in them, either. Maybe one at the beginning of each chapter.* Well, what a revelation this had been. He didn't just write picture books, he wrote all kinds of stories.

She desperately wanted to read the other two series, but how could she ask him without him knowing she'd been snooping around in his email. *I suppose it serves me right for being so nosey, to be tormented by the knowledge of those other series.* She closed out the emails and sat back in his chair.

Her eyes kept drifting back to those emails with the children's books in them. God, she wished he'd send them to his agent and editor. *I know they would love them as much as I do.* Why was he so darn stubborn about this? Couldn't he see the talent he had? Her hand itched to hit send on those two emails.

No, it's time for a shower, she clicked back to his normal email account and took her coffee cup into the kitchen and put it in the dishwasher. She marched down the hall to the bathroom. The whole time she washed her mind reeled with possibilities. *If he just sent them, I know they would love them. And he would start to believe in himself as an author—not just some guy riding the wave of popularity.* She was certain his life and attitude would change forever, and in a good way. Maybe she could just continue to nag him into it.

When the water started to cool, she wondered if she'd even washed. She felt soapy and her hair felt sudsy, so maybe she'd done it on auto-pilot. She rinsed off and got out, put a towel around her head and another around her body and marched down the hall to his studio. She brought back up the email, clicked on his pen name, and clicked send on the two emails for the series she'd read.

And then she panicked. He was going to kill her. *Oh, my God, what have I done? He's going to be furious!* She ran back to his bedroom, threw on her clean work clothes, put the towels in the hamper, and ran out the door. She drove directly to work and just started working like a woman possessed. How could she have done that? What was she going to say to him?

"Hey, boss. I thought you weren't coming in until lunch. That's another couple of hours away." Cindy wrapped the silverware into napkins.

"Oh, well, I changed my mind." She waved her hand in the air and started scrubbing the salad bar. It didn't really need scrubbing, but it was getting it anyway. She'd clearly lost her mind this morning.

By the time lunch rolled around and Jeremy would be walking in the door any minute, she was sick to her stomach. When he did finally come in about two, he had a huge grin on his face and was followed by Hank, Trey, and Owen. She was so excited to see Owen, everything else fled her mind.

She rushed over to Owen and gave him a huge bear hug, to the point that he actually grunted from being squeezed. She stepped back and grinned up at him with her hands on his arms. "I've been so worried about you. Are you okay?"

"Um, I'm fine. You're not mad at me?" He frowned. "I, uh, caused a fire."

"Did you do it deliberately?"

He clenched his jaw and his hands tightened into fists. "No, but if I hadn't been here it wouldn't have happened."

She patted his arm. "Owen, it was an accident, and accidents happen to everyone."

"But…"

"No buts. All of you come sit down. Let's get you some lunch, on the house." She grabbed menus and led them over to a table.

Jeremy said quietly to Amber, "Nolan and Greg will be joining us, just to wrap up the paperwork. I've filled them in."

She nodded and steered the group to a larger table. Amber called out to Cindy who was watching the proceedings with rapt attention. "I'm going to sit down with the guys, please come take their orders. There will be seven of us"

Cindy nodded, got a few more menus, a tray of ice waters, and hurried over. Cindy took their drink orders and Amber told her to include Greg and Nolan's preferred choices.

Greg and Nolan walked in within seconds of each other and joined the table. Amber was glad the lunch rush was over and they had the restaurant to themselves.

Greg nodded to the table and spoke to Owen. "Good to see you, Owen. It's been a few years. You remember me, don't you? I'm Greg Jones. My family lived next to your family. I was just a punk kid when you left for the Air Force. Glad to see you back home."

Owen nodded at Greg and looked at Nolan. "Am I under arrest for the fire, officer?"

"Nope, not unless you set it on purpose or Amber wants to press charges. Let's order some lunch and you can tell me what happened."

Owen nodded and Cindy came back over with their drinks and took their lunch orders. Even though it was after two, both Greg and Nolan ordered. Amber assumed that was to put Owen at ease, because she was fairly certain they would have had lunch by now. Their kindness warmed her heart.

Nolan said to Owen, "Tell me what happened the night of the fire."

Owen looked at Amber. "I'm so sorry."

She patted his hand. "It's okay, just tell Nolan what happened."

"Well, I was all settled in for the night. I'd had the dinner Amber left for me and had just finished my chip snack. I'm not a big sweets eater—I like a bag of chips for my dessert. So, I was just finishing the last chip and I heard a weird noise outside. I peeked out the window but couldn't see anything because there was a little glow from the space heater and the emergency lights over the doors. So, I dropped the chip bag and let go of the curtain. I wondered later if the curtain got caught on the space heater. At the time, I was just concerned about the noise. I grabbed my backpack in case I needed something out of it. I went out the door and walked all around looking for what might have caused the noise, and making sure everything was secure. I walked up and down the block some making sure no one was breaking in. You know, like had happened earlier in the summer when that kid was breaking into places after getting burned out of his house."

Nolan nodded.

"So, when I got done looking around I went back to the restaurant and saw some smoke, so I stood to the side and opened up the door, and it did that backdraft thing. You know, like they showed on that movie where flame leaps out the door. Well, that made me think of being in the war. I looked inside after the backdraft flames stopped and everything was on fire. I was discharged after we had something like that happen, and a couple of guys were killed who were too close to the door. So, I panicked and ran away."

Nolan nodded.

"And after I ran away, then I thought about how mad it would make Amber that I burned up her restaurant, and I also got scared for her because she lived upstairs and I didn't know whether to run farther or go back and save her. But I decided to go back. When I got back, she was sitting in a Jeep and the fire department was there, so I ran away again, because I was afraid to go to jail. And I didn't want to see Amber mad at me."

Amber patted his arm again. "I wasn't mad. I knew you would never do anything to hurt me on purpose."

"But my carelessness caused the fire, and what if it killed you?"

"It didn't kill me and the fire suppression system kept the rest of the restaurant safe, along with the fire department coming so fast. Jeremy found me and brought me out and put me in his Jeep. Everything is okay." She looked at Nolan and then Greg. "Right?"

"Yes," Nolan said, "it was clearly an accident."

Greg nodded.

Hank cleared his throat. "Owen, I want you to come out to the ranch. You can live in one of the outbuildings, or you can come on the payroll and live in the bunk house."

"Naw, Hank. I don't know anything about ranching. I

wouldn't be any help, just a hindrance. And I can't just live in one of your buildings 'cause I can't pay rent."

"I don't need rent, but I do need someone to keep an eye on things out there in the outbuildings. Nothing fancy. Just keep a lookout for trouble, and if you find some you come back and tell me what's going on. For helping me out, you can live in the building, and I'll stock it with food. That would keep me from having to hire another hand."

"Well, I don't want to be any trouble. But if you need a pair of eyes and ears, that I have."

Hank nodded. "It's a deal."

Everyone went their separate ways and Amber was so happy about finding Owen that she didn't remember about sending Jeremy's series to his publisher and agent for over an hour. And then she started to worry again.

CHAPTER
thirty-four

JEREMY WAS HIGH ON ACCOMPLISHMENT when he got home. What a great day this was! He dug right in to work on his graphic novel. But he kept thinking about seeing Amber's face when Owen walked in behind him. She'd been so relieved and excited to see him, and hadn't held any type of grudge for the fire, even though the rebuild was going to give her a lot more work and responsibility. She'd not held the slightest bit of anger—he wasn't sure if he would have been so generous. She could have died from smoke inhalation and she'd lost business, and what if the insurance adjuster had followed through on his threats? No, he didn't think he would be nearly as kind as she was.

The trek in to find Owen hadn't been easy. They'd taken horses into a hard to reach area to search. Owen must have thought no one would find him because he was just sitting at his campsite until they rode in. He'd tried to run but Hank had stopped him with a firm command. He'd had his rope out if he'd needed it, but Owen had responded to the authority in Hank's voice.

He'd stopped and listened to them as they explained that Amber was worried about him—not angry, just worried. They'd made it sound like Owen needed to come into town to make sure her name was cleared, and that's all it took. He wasn't about to let her be in trouble for his actions. He was a good guy, down deep. Jeremy was darn glad Hank had the foresight to take four horses with them so Owen would have one to ride down. None of them were little guys and two of them sharing one horse would not have been pretty.

Jeremy looked back down at his drawing. Still smiling at the thought of them sharing horses, he wanted to tell Amber about it—maybe tonight if she came over or he went to see her, she would get a kick out of the idea. He got a new piece of paper and drew up a caricature of them sharing horses and titled it "The Rescue of Owen".

He texted her asking if she wanted to come over after work tonight, he had something to show her. Then he went back to work on his graphic novel. She might not get back to him for a while if she was busy working.

AMBER GOT A text from Jeremy. He'd sent it a couple of hours ago, but she'd been working. One of her servers had called in sick so she was covering for her. She thought about ignoring it, but she just couldn't, so she clicked on the text.

Jeremy: Want to come over tonight, after work? I have something to show you.

Fear rose up in her and she thought she might faint.

Amber: Something good or something bad.

Jeremy: Good silly what would be bad.

Amber: Oh nothing, just checking. One of my staff didn't show tonight so I'm pulling double duty

Jeremy: So do you want to come, or are you going to be too tired?

Amber: I'll come.

She decided it might be the last time he wanted to see her, once he found out what she'd done. So, she decided to take advantage of the invitation and pray he didn't open his email. She had no idea how long it would take them to get back to him. Probably a few days, at least. After she closed the restaurant she went up and changed into a sweater and jeans and grabbed some clothes for overnight.

When she got to Jeremy's house, she knocked and when he didn't answer she used her key and walked into the house toward his studio. He was sitting at his computer, but she saw the cutest picture titled "The Rescue of Owen". He'd drawn the four big men on two horses that were groaning under the weight of two men each. The horses had sweat spraying around them and their legs were buckling.

She laughed. "Jeremy, this is awesome."

She turned toward him and he looked up at her with an expression that made her blood run cold.

"How could you?"

"Let me explain." She couldn't tell if he was furious or devastated.

"Explain what exactly? Stabbing me in the back? Taking my work that I told you I didn't want submitted and sending it in without my permission? While I was out doing you a favor? Looking for the homeless guy you were worried about. I've spent nearly two weeks trying to find him and you pay me back with deception and treachery."

"No, Jeremy. They're such good books, the world needs them."

"Yeah, right. And I suppose you did it for me. Like I need more money."

"It's not about money," she said quietly.

"Get out, Amber. I don't even want to see you again and leave the key. I've had enough scheming women in my life, just coming and going as they please. I don't need another one."

"I'm not another scheming woman. I love you and want you to understand what talent you have and to know how valuable you and your creativity are."

"Get out. Now."

"Jeremy," she pleaded.

"Get. Out. Now."

"Fine, be a stubborn ass, who doesn't believe in himself. What do I care." She put down the picture and dropped his key on top of it. Before she walked out, she turned to him. "I hope someday, someone will get it through that thick skull of yours that it's not all about money. You have a great talent that you should be sharing with the world instead of hiding in the bottom of your filing cabinet. You're a coward, Jeremy. And a damn fool." She turned and walked out of his life.

She fumed all the way home. Stupid man, not even willing to try. She knew she had no right to send in his books—that was just wrong on every level and she would have apologized profusely if he'd given her half a chance. She'd been wrong sending in his work. But if he had not been such a chicken himself and sent it in, she wouldn't have been tempted to do it. If he'd even talked to her about it, maybe explained why he didn't want to—but no. It was just drop it, Amber. Well, she didn't want to drop it. He had an amazing talent and owed it to the world to share it.

Jeremy was furious. How dare she send in his stories. Now, he was going to get email back ripping them to shreds and ripping his childhood memories right along with them. He wasn't a coward, he knew what he was doing. She didn't know anything about publishing and the heartache it could bring. Of course, he hadn't exactly explained it all to her, so she would understand. But still, she had no business butting into his business. And to think he'd entertained notions about them making a life together, no fricken way was *that* going to happen.

The very first time he left her alone in his house and trusted her and this is the way she repays him? Nice. And then she didn't tell him she'd even done it—she could have mentioned it before he saw the auto-emails his publisher and agent always sent for submissions.

Interfering, pain in the ass woman. Thinks she knows better. Well, she was wrong. He knew better. He'd sent in a book of his own a long time ago and both his agent and publisher had basically patted him on the head and told him not to quit his day job. Which was writing the Tsilly books that they controlled. So now, he wrote his other stories for himself and himself alone. He'd known it wasn't a good idea to let Amber read them.

Thinking back on the humiliation of that rejection so many years ago still stung. He'd loved that story and he'd been so excited to share it. The publisher had said he needed more experience and that the market wasn't open to the story he'd written. It had been about a kid that was a super hero. There were all kinds of books about that now, so why was his not good enough?

His agent had told him that it wasn't good to split his focus because he was so new to the authors' world and he needed to hone his craft. Well, that was over ten years ago and he didn't feel any different about his 'craft' skills. *And just to prove it to myself I'm going to find that book and read it.*

Jeremy looked until he found the book he'd written

shortly after high school graduation, and started reading. He wasn't two pages in when he saw some glaring issues. Okay, so he had learned some things about his craft since that time. He continued to read his first story and realized that, in fact, he'd learned a lot. He might like to redo it with what he'd learned—it would be fun to see the difference between now and then.

He got out the series Amber had sent in—to see what they looked like in comparison. He found them pretty solid, he saw a couple of things he would change in the wording, things he'd learned—but not a lot of them. These were only a couple of years old, he'd obviously learned a lot in the interim from his first book to this series.

Maybe they *would* like the series she sent. Well he didn't have any choice now. He would get feedback eventually. He was damn glad it didn't have his name on it, though. It might take months with it going into the slush pile, but he would hear back. He would just have to suck it up and take it like a man.

CHAPTER
thirty-five

KIMBERLY MARCHED INTO AMBER'S office, shut the door, and put her hands on her hips. "Just what in the hell is going on around here? You've been cranky as a raccoon with no water to wash his food in."

"A raccoon? Seriously?"

"Have you ever seen a cranky raccoon?"

"No." Amber shook her head.

"Well, I have. And let me tell you, they can get really mean."

"I'll have to take your word for that, I suppose." Amber realized she had a scowl on her face and tried to ease it into a smile, but it felt more like a grimace.

"Back to the question, why are you so damn cranky? Does it have something to do with Jeremy not coming in for the last week?"

"I am not cranky." The scowl was back, she could feel it.

Kimberly raised one eyebrow.

"Fine, I might be a little out of sorts, which is why I'm in my office rather than out with the customers."

"And the fact that Jeremy hasn't been in about the same length of time you've been cranky?"

Amber sighed. "Yes. Well he is mad at me. I overstepped my bounds and did something he's very angry about. So, yes. I suppose his absence has something to do with my out of sorts-ness."

"Why don't you just call him and apologize?"

"I have called. I have left him messages, and I sent email. I'm not sure this is something he will ever forgive me for. Besides that, I'm not fully convinced it wasn't necessary."

"Sounds interesting."

"Yes, but completely confidential, which was the problem in the first place. So, I'm not saying another word about it." She shut her mouth with finality.

"I'm not asking until it gets resolved, and then I want all the deets."

"Did you miss the part where I said it won't ever be resolved?"

Kimberly shrugged. "Oh, sure it will. The man can only stand to eat pizza and Korean Bar-B-Q so long, before he'll need to come back here to eat."

"He can also go to the resort and the amusement park restaurants."

"But they don't have your chocolate French silk pie," Kimberly shot over her shoulder as she walked out of the office.

Amber frowned, not sure he would care, or if he would ever want to eat her specialty again.

JEREMY HAD THE first half of the graphic novel done and he decided he wanted to let Beth read it and give him some feedback. So, after he okayed it with Hank he drove over to the ranch to give it to her. He got there before the bus would drop her off, because he was sick and tired of his own company. It had been a week since Amber had broken his trust and smashed it into tiny little pieces, and he'd kept to himself most of that time. He'd picked up food from various restaurants and even cooked himself some things, when he didn't feel like getting out. But now, he was ready to see a few more people.

When he drove into the ranch, there wasn't anyone around and school wouldn't be out for about an hour, so he decided to drive out to the cabin Owen was staying in to see how he was doing. When he got close to the building, he was surprised to see it dark inside and no smoke coming out of the chimney. It was cool up here in the mountains. A fire would help with the chill. He got out of his Jeep, walked up to the door and knocked.

He heard Owen call out, "It's open." So, he walked into the gloom.

He looked around and was surprised to find Owen sitting on the floor of the main room near the picture window, with a small stack of blankets around him. The rest of the room didn't look like it had been touched.

"What's going on here, buddy?"

"I'm not anyone's buddy, and I'm here keeping an eye out for Hank. Just like he asked me to."

Okay, a little on the extreme side. "Yes, but it doesn't look like you're living in the cabin much. There's no fire in the fireplace or lights on, and are you sleeping on the floor?"

"Yes, that way I can be by the window to see what's going on."

Jeremy sat down on the sofa so he wasn't looming over Owen. "I don't think Hank was worried about twenty-four-seven monitoring, just someone in the house to keep a light eye on things. I'm certain he expected you to sleep in the bed and use the rest of the cabin as a home."

"Naw, I don't want to mess it up."

What is this crazy talk? "Owen, it's a cabin to live in and use."

"It's too nice, I don't want to muck it up."

This wasn't the Taj Mahal, what was he worried about. "What do you mean muck it up."

"I'm just a homeless drifter, Jeremy."

"Owen, you're more than that, you've lived in a house

before and know how to take care of one. When you were a kid you lived in one of the nicest ones in town."

"That was a long time ago," Owen muttered.

"So long you can't remember how to build a fire in the fireplace and make a bed? Maybe wash a dish or two?"

"Of course, I remember those things. I just don't deserve to be living here."

Okay, this martyr act was starting to piss him off. "That's bullshit, Owen. You're a vet. You fought for our country. You kept us safe."

"Not everyone sees it that way."

"Who gives a rat's ass what some people think. There is always going to be someone who doesn't like what you do. But that doesn't mean you have to stop doing it, or you should be ashamed of it. Naysayers be damned. There are a lot of people that are grateful for your service."

Owen shook his head. "Funny thing is, Amber said nearly the same thing to me, the night before I almost burned her to a crisp. If she hadn't helped me to start believing in myself, I wouldn't have gone out looking for what was making that noise and I wouldn't have caught her place on fire. I'm a fuck-up, Jeremy."

Amber. Of course, she'd been trying to help Owen. And wasn't he the hypocrite telling Owen to ignore the naysayers? Fine, he was a hypocrite, but he damn well wasn't leaving Owen like this. "Oh, please. That was an accident and maybe you going out there saved Amber from something a lot worse. Did you ever think of that? What if someone was going to rob her or hurt her and you scared them off? Now stop acting like a dumb ass and get a fire started in here, and some light on. Take a shower, make food, sleep in the bed, stop acting like a martyr, and live your life. Amber would be pissed off if she saw you living like this."

He chuckled. "Yeah, you have a point, the woman doesn't take kindly to people feeling sorry for themselves."

Jeremy rubbed the back of his neck. "No, she doesn't." Damn, here he was handing out advice he probably should be following himself and the catalyst was Amber—right in the middle of both.

Jeremy dropped off the book for Beth to read and went home, thinking about what he'd said to Owen. He still wasn't certain how he felt about the whole thing with Amber—he still felt betrayed by her actions, but she might have a point about him being a coward by not sending in his new work. He decided to check email and not think about it.

He had an email from his agent with the subject line: Busted! He groaned and clicked on the email.

Jeremy I know you coached this new author Allen Andrews, where did you meet him anyway? Some conference? Book signing?

How can I tell you ask? Because he is already following my protocol on submissions and no one knows those protocols except for my published authors, even then most of them only follow bits and pieces of them. You and a couple of romance authors are the only ones that follow them to a T. So, since these are children's books, you've got to be the one that did it.

Thanks! He seems to be an excellent author, some of the phrasing could be tightened up, but other than that they are great stories. I have every intention of taking him on. I suppose you also suggested he pitch them to your publisher, they would be a fool not to take him, so if he submitted it's probably a done deal.

If you find any other authors of the same caliber feel free to pass them on. Next time, have them put in a mention that you sent them, you've got good taste.

And just so you don't think I'm getting soft... How's the graphic novel coming?

Trisha

Well, shit. Then Amber had to go and be right about his books. Damn he was going to have to do some groveling. He could feel it coming.

CHAPTER
thirty-six

AMBER WAS FINALLY STARTING TO feel less cranky. It had only been two weeks since her blowup with Jeremy, but she had decided to move on with her life and quit moping about some guy that was too stupid to see how fantastic she was. Yes, she'd made a mistake—even a rather big mistake. But if he really loved her, he would at least listen and give her a chance to apologize. So, she was just going to move on and forget all about him.

She almost dropped a tray of drinks when Owen walked in. He was cleaned up and had a haircut. He walked into her restaurant and sat at the counter and picked up the menu, like he was going to order. Very interesting, indeed. She was glad it was past the lunch rush so she would have time to talk to him a bit.

She finished with the table she was giving drinks to and went over behind the counter, down to where Owen was sitting. "Hi, Owen. It's so good to see you."

"It's good to see you, too, Amber. I came for lunch and to chat with you for a few minutes."

She grinned. "That's great. Do you know what you want to order?"

"Yes, I'll have the fried chicken dinner and a glass of iced tea."

"Let me get that ordered and then we can talk."

She brought back the iced tea and set it down in front of him.

"So, I just wanted to thank you for all you've done for me."

"Oh, I didn't—"

"Stop and let me say what I came here to say." She nodded so he continued. "I was living in the woods for a couple of years all alone, barely surviving. Fishing and gathering wild fruits and vegetables. Living in a makeshift lean-to, fortunately we have pretty mild winters down at the lower elevations, so I didn't have too much trouble with snow and rain.

"Then the fires started and I had to evacuate the area I was living in. Trey and his crew didn't even realize I was living there because I was just barely living at all. When I came into town, I was hiding in the area where my family had lived before. I knew all the hiding spots since I'd found them as a child and teenager. I was eating out of your dumpster and then you caught me and offered me a place to sleep and be warm.

"When your place caught on fire, you didn't blame me. You sent Hank and Trey and Jeremy out to find me. Hank gave me a place to stay, but I was still living like a homeless person until about a week ago, when Jeremy came and told me to stop feeling sorry for myself and get my act together. He also mentioned that you would not be happy to know how I was subsisting, and I had to agree with him."

Jeremy had gone out to talk to Owen? Well, that was something anyway. She didn't think he'd been to town much in the two weeks.

"So, I went up to the ranch house and hired on as a hand. I'm living in the bunk-house and working a job and acting like a real person. Hank helped me get some new clothes and a haircut. He fronted me some of my salary so I could come into town and get a meal and talk with you. He also put me on his health insurance and I saw Doc Sorenson for a physical this morning. He suggested I do some counseling with Pastor Davidson, the elder one."

"Owen, I'm so glad to hear this." She reached out and held his hand. Her throat was so tight she could barely speak.

He patted her hand. "You were the catalyst for all of it, so I just wanted to say thank you for treating me like a real person and not just a homeless bum."

"Anyone would—"

"No, not anyone and not everyone, either. But you did and I appreciate it."

"I was honored to do a small thing for someone who has fought for and defended our country. I feel like we all owe you a debt of gratitude." Her eyes filled with tears and she tried to blink them away.

"Well, I didn't see it much that way and I appreciate you standing by me. Jeremy kind of said the same thing."

"Good for Jeremy. It was my pleasure and I hope you come in and see me every so often. I kind of miss our talks."

"I will. I miss them too."

Cindy brought over his fried chicken and his eyes lit up with pleasure. "I like living with and working for Hank, but we eat a lot of beef and I'm happy to have some chicken. Guess that's the price you pay for working on a cattle ranch—gotta support the company."

Cindy and Amber laughed. Amber said, "You come in for chicken any time you like. We'll always have some waiting for you."

"Thanks, now I'm going to eat this deliciousness and not be talking too much, so if you ladies have something to do, I won't be lonely if you leave me."

Amber looked at Cindy. "I think that's a hint the man would like to eat in peace."

Owen winked at her and stuffed a big bite of fried chicken and mashed potatoes in his mouth.

JEREMY HAD BEEN thinking a lot about his reluctance to tell his agent and publisher about his secret identity. His agent had emailed Allen Andrews and had said she would like to talk to him. He put her off, but couldn't do so forever. So he sat down at his computer to come clean and saw another new email in his Allen Andrews inbox. This one was from his publisher. They were very interested in purchasing his books and wondered if he have an agent.

He shook his head. "Guess I'll be coming clean with both of the Terrible T's at the same time," he muttered and opened a new email under that same account, directed to both his agent and editor. He told them Allen Andrews was a pseudonym and that he was happy they liked his series, and he would be pleased to work with them both, on this new series. Oh, and by the way, he also had a chapter book series for grade school kids and a YA series if they would like to look at them also. Then he sat back and waited for the explosion.

It didn't take long.

His phone rang within five minutes of sending the email. His agent. He answered it.

"This is Jeremy Allen Scott."

"Dammit, Jeremy. How long have you been holding out on me?" Trisha demanded.

"Not holding out exactly. Just not sharing."

"Jeremy, that series is going to rock the children's publishing industry. Every single child in America and every single adult, as well, has done at least one of the things in those books. People are going to see their childhood in them and buy them like hotcakes. Why the hell were you not sharing?"

"I just didn't plan to share them. I wrote them for myself."

"Well to hell with that. Why did you send them in then?" she asked.

"I didn't. I let a friend read them and she loved them and she went behind my back to email them to you."

"Well, I need her address so I can start sending her flowers every week for the rest of her life."

"Isn't that a little over the top, even for you, Trish?"

"No, Jeremy. It's not." She said with all seriousness.

His phone beeped and he looked at the screen. Tony. Great. Just great. He told Trisha, "Tony's on the other line."

"Fine, I am going to hang up. You tell him to call me—do not discuss this with him. This is what you pay me for. And as soon as you hang up—send the other two series."

"Yes, ma'am," he said to dead air and then switched to the other line.

"Hey, Tony."

"Dammit, Jeremy. How long have you been holding out on me?" Tony shouted.

"Oh, for Pete's sake. That's exactly what Trisha said. She wants you to call her."

"Fine, I will. And send me the other two series *right now*, while I negotiate with your agent."

"Yes, sir," he said to dead air. He sighed and put his phone down, pulled up the emails with the other two series and pushed send on all of them. "In for a penny, in for a pound," he muttered.

CHAPTER
thirty-seven

J EREMY SPENT THE NEXT WEEK negotiating with the Terrible T's. They had a few changes for the children's book, but they were pretty much the same ones he'd noted when he'd done the read through. So, they didn't bother him in the least. In fact, he fixed a couple of areas they hadn't mentioned and re-sent them. They decided to publish one every four months, which would mean a two-year publishing schedule.

They also decided to wait at least eight months before they revealed who Allen Andrews really was. Finally, they decided to stagger the publications of the other two series, so that he was publishing a book every two months and that didn't count the Tsilly books or the graphic novel.

They were still deciding if he should use pseudonyms

for the other two series or publish them all under Allen Andrews. Too many different genres under the same name could confuse people, but the momentum built by all of them would push sales in the other categories. So, they were doing some market research and asking a focus group. He was not a fan of focus groups, but figured they might come in handy on this issue.

Jeremy decided it was also time to talk to Amber. She'd been right about all of it and he needed to admit he was wrong. He also hoped he could get her back as his girlfriend or even something more. He needed to do this one up big. Yes, she shouldn't have sent them in without his permission, but he'd also been somewhat of a chicken-shit about it and had needed the kick in the ass. He spent the whole day thinking about what to do to make it up to her. Maybe he should call in reinforcements.

He finally decided on a plan and asked some of the volunteer firefighters to help him with it. They were always game for things like this.

∞

AMBER WAS IN the soon-to-be wedding reception venue, Marc was showing her what they had done so far. All the burned out material was gone and they had the foundation extended for the added-on areas, and had started framing the different rooms, so she could see the layout. He'd also gotten some guys upstairs to begin the renovations. It all looked like a big mess to her, but Marc was excited, so she knew it was going to be great.

Marc said, "Amber you'll need to start thinking about light fixtures and wall colors and all the many other details. We don't need them today, but even toilets come in a lot of different varieties, and all these things will need to be decided on. You might even want to get someone to help you with the decisions, because it can be overwhelming."

"You don't just have some standard stuff you can put in?"

"No, not really, which is why I'm mentioning it now. You'll need to order everything shipped in. I can send you some websites to get started thinking about things. Is there anyone you might like to have in on the decisions?"

She shook her head. "I can't think of a single person who would give a crap about this at all, let alone want to help make decisions—including myself."

"I have a suggestion of someone."

"Who?"

"Sheila. She's the type of person who would revel in this. You could have her do a first pass on the items, and have her give you, say, three to five options, and then you could make the final decisions without having to wade through a thousand toilets, for example."

"A thousand toilets? You're exaggerating, right?" Why in the hell would there be a thousand different toilets? He had to be pulling her leg.

"Nope, not at all."

"Oh, dear God. I'll call Sheila and see if she's interested. Thanks for the heads up. I think."

Marc chuckled. "My pleasure, but better now when you have plenty of time than having to make thousands of decisions at crunch time."

"I guess so. Leaving now before my head explodes." She turned to go.

"Let me know if you want Sheila CC'd on the websites."

She didn't look back. She just waived her hand to acknowledge his request. Thousands of decisions with a thousand or more options per decision? Yeah, there was no way she wanted to do that alone. She'd work with anyone, even the devil himself, to avoid that. Jeremy's ex wasn't nearly as scary as all those choices.

Her cell phone had Sheila's number in it after the different meetings, so she scrolled through the contact list until she found it and pushed send.

"Hi, Amber."

"Hello, Sheila. So I was wondering if you could be my construction assistant."

"Sure, how can I help?"

"Don't you want to know what it is first?" Amber would never answer a blanket request like that.

"No, I just want to help anyway I can."

She pulled the phone away from her ear and looked at it, like who is this woman. "Good. Well, what I need is some help making all the decisions to outfit the new construction. I was thinking you could give each choice a first pass and then give me your top three picks, so I can choose between them."

"Ohhh, that sounds like so much fun."

Amber felt her eyebrows rise. "It does?"

"Oh, yes. I would love doing that."

"Good. I'll have Marc send you some websites and lists of what kinds of things need to be decided on first. Did you know he said there were a thousand toilets to choose from?"

"Sure. One piece, two piece, tankless, concealed tank, lever flush, button flush, no touch flush, low profile, high profile. Yep, lots of choices."

Shit, he hadn't been joking. She still had held out hope he had been. Sheila just smashed that idea to pieces. "Okay, then. You can expect to see some emails from Marc."

"Goody. I can plan to meet with you every day, if you want, after your lunch rush."

Every day? Oh, hell no. There was no way she was giving this that much of her time. "I think once or twice a week should be enough. Let's start with once a week. Come by after two, when you have something for me to look at."

"Will do. Thanks for asking me to help, Amber."

"You're welcome and thanks for being willing to."

With Sheila's help, she could at least breathe again. It was still going to be a pain in the neck, but she could handle it. She hoped.

CHAPTER
thirty-eight

J EREMY WAS NERVOUS. WHAT IF Amber thought this was stupid? Or more importantly, what if it embarrassed her, or even pissed her off? He'd gotten the firefighters involved. Which included Chris and he hadn't thought she would be irritated by it, but sometimes siblings weren't as in tune with each other as they thought they were.

He wasn't going to let fear stop him, however. He was going after the woman he loved and was going to hope like hell she wanted him, too. The alternative was unthinkable—she was part of his heart and he wanted to build a life with her. They fit and formed a family unit— and that was worth everything. He hadn't had a family in a very long time.

He got the text from Barbara, looked around, and squared his shoulders. "Let's do this, then."

"Ten-four," Greg said over the radio. "Let's move."

Pumper One went first. Chris drove it to just past Amber's restaurant. The ladder truck went second. It would take the longest to setup, but it needed to be in the middle for the best impact. Greg parked it out in the street across from Amber's restaurant. Engine Two brought up the rear and Terry parked it behind the other two. They stabilized the aerial apparatus and raised the ladder—not the full extent, but far enough to hang the display. They set up the other four displays, on the ground next to the trucks. When everything was ready, they used the air horn on the pumper to get everyone's attention.

Jeremy stood on the top of the ladder truck below the display board. She wouldn't be able to punch him in the nose that way, if she felt so inclined. People gathered all around. Finally, Amber came out of the restaurant trailed by Barbara and Kristen, the decoys.

When everyone was gathered around, Jeremy used the loudspeaker. "Hello, friends and neighbors. I'm here to publicly confess that I've been behaving in a cowardly fashion and to turn over a new leaf. You see, below me a depiction of the Tsilly Adventure books that I've been writing since I was in high school." He gestured to his right to indicate the 6x4 foot plywood board he'd drawn one of the Tsilly covers on. "It's been a great career and will continue to be, but I've always felt like it was Sandy's talent and imagination and I was just the hand that drew it for her."

Amber put her hands on her hips and frowned at him. He smiled down at her and continued speaking.

"The game company has asked me to expand the books to include graphic novels and I have decided to do that as well. Here is the cover for the first one." He gestured to his left and Chris pulled the covering off the board to reveal the six-foot cover. A general murmur of excitement spread through the crowd and some of the older kids were vocal about their approval.

When the roar died down, Jeremy continued speaking. "This has been a fun project and did stretch me, but again, it is based on Sandy's stories. Not my own ideas." Amber crossed her arms and glared at him tapping her foot.

He continued, "However I have, in the past, written several other series that were all my own idea and creativity, but I was too much of a chicken-shit to send them in. But one day, I did finally let someone read one of them, and that was Amber. She loved them, and encouraged me to send them in, but I refused, stating all the reasons why that wasn't a good idea. Well, Amber didn't buy my BS, so she sent the series in that I let her read. I was furious, of course, since I was terrified of rejection." Now half the crowd had folded their arms and were glaring at him, too. It appeared the whole town thought he was a damn fool. Well, he couldn't blame them when he agreed with them.

"Anyway, the publishers didn't hate them." Now the crowd was looking at him like 'Well duh'. "Now, before I can go on, I need you all to promise me something. You all have to promise not to let one peep of this information out of town. Not on social media, not in phone calls, no pictures, no texts, nothing. Can you do that?"

"Yes," they roared.

"Okay. Then raise your right hand and repeat after me. We promise to keep this information to ourselves until we are given permission from Jeremy."

They laughed and then repeated his words. "Good, thanks, now the reason for the secrecy is that I'm going to be publishing my own unique work under a pseudonym, and we are not going to let it be known it's me for eight months. To let it gain its own foothold before the Tsilly followers are alerted." Everyone nodded at that explanation.

"I have a series for young adults, the first cover for that is over by Engine Two." Terry pulled the cloth off and some of the young adults in the crowd cheered and moved over toward it to get a closer look. "I also have a series of chapter books; you can see the first in that group next to Pumper One." He gestured toward that one and Chris pulled the tarp off. "Last, but not least, is the series Amber sent in, which is above my head. It's a children's picture book series in the same genre as the Tsilly books." He pulled the wrapper off so everyone could see the depiction.

After everyone had ample time to view it, Jeremy said, "And now for the dedication that will appear in this first book." Jeremy reached above his head and swiveled the picture to the back where it read:

Dedication

To Amber, for her faith in me and her stubbornness

not to allow me to hide my light under a basket, or in this case inside a filing cabinet.

Thank you so much for your conviction and determination.

I love you.

Everyone gasped and he looked down at Amber. She still had her arms folded across her chest and he had no idea what she was thinking. She looked up at him and then turned and walked back into the restaurant.

He looked over to Chris, who pointed at the door—for him to follow her.

AMBER WAS IN shock. What in the hell was Jeremy doing? Had he lost his mind? Yes, she'd called him a coward, but that didn't mean he had to go nuts. She went into her office and collapsed on a chair. She put her arms on her knees and her face in her hands. Her thoughts were whirling.

Her hands were pulled away from her face and there he was kneeling in front of her. "I'm sorry. Did I embarrass you? I just wanted to show you I wasn't afraid anymore. I just wanted you to know that I appreciate what you did, for the length you went to. I just wanted you to know that I love you and want you to be part of my life. I'm sorry if it was too much."

She put her hands on his face. "Jeremy, all I needed was a phone call. I love you, too."

He looked at her in confusion and then a slow smile spread across his face. "Then, you forgive me?"

"Of course, I do. I was at fault, too."

"But in the best possible way."

She felt a crooked smile on her face. "Maybe."

"Then, you'll marry me? You'll be my family?"

If he'd asked her that question before their breakup, she would have run in the other direction, terrified. But the weeks she'd been without him had shown her just what he meant to her. They were good together. She nodded decisively. "Yes, I will."

He kissed her then, long and slow. Her temperature rose. She pulled him closer and reveled in his taste, in his scent, in his warmth. She could kiss him for a week or two.

He drew back and pulled a piece of paper out of his jacket pocket. "Good, because your new menu would look pretty silly otherwise."

She unfolded the paper. It was the same as her current menu except there, next to her restaurant, was Jeremy, just as he was before, only this time he was holding her hand. She saw in the top corner was a new tree that had their initials carved in it.

She smiled at him. "It's perfect."

The End

Printed in Poland
by Amazon Fulfillment
Poland Sp. z o.o., Wrocław